The
Five

M. Drury IV

Amsterdam is _not_ in
Germany. Nor do they
speak German. Try
the Netherlands, where
they speak Dutch.

DEDICATION

To my amazing mother and my wonderful husband, without whom I would not still exist. To Julia and Kelly, for being my sounding boards and for hyping me up always. Last, but not least, to my cat, Beignet. He can't read.

MY DEAREST DEMETER,

    I DO NOT WRITE TO YOU IN SEARCH OF FORGIVENESS. I KNOW I WILL NOT FIND IT. MY SINS ARE MY OWN, AND I, ALONE, MUST ATONE FOR THEM. I WRITE ONLY TO INFORM YOU OF THE TRAGEDY TO COME. I KNOW IT IS NOT WHAT YOU WOULD LIKE TO HEAR, BUT YOU MUST TAKE HEED, FOR THE DOWNFALL OF ALL WILL COME IF YOU DO NOT. THE MOMENTS NOW ARE FLEETING AND ALL TOO SOON I WILL BE GONE. HOWEVER, AS I WATCH THE WAVES CRASH UNDER THE SETTING SUN, YOU ARE THE ONLY ONE I FIND CONCERN FOR.

    I CAN FIND HUMOR IN THE IRONY I AM CHARGED WITH TREASON AGAINST THE GODS, WHILE THE BLOOD IS ON THEIR HANDS. I HAVE SPOKEN TO THE FATES, AND THEY HAVE REVEALED THE PROPHECY TO ME.

'THE MIGHTY GOD WILL BETRAY US ALL, AND EVERY BEING WILL SURELY FALL
FILLED WITH PRIDE, AND FILLED WITH GREED, NO ONE WHO FIGHTS HIM ALONE CAN SUCCEED.
IN THESSALY, THE CHILDREN OF MYTHS WILL SEE A PATH SHALL FORGE BENEATH THEIR FEET.
THE ISLE OF EXTINCTION IS THE JOURNEY'S END, WHERE FRIEND IS FOE, AND FOE IS FRIEND.
A WEAPON IS FORGED WHEN THE BLOOD DOES ARRIVE, AND THE MIGHTY WILL FALL BY THE HANDS OF THE FIVE.'

    IT IS ON YOUR SHOULDERS NOW, A TRUTH I REGRET. YOU MUST FIND THE FIVE, FOR THEY ARE THE ONLY ONES WHO WOULD PREVAIL. THE FIVE MUST BEGIN THEIR JOURNEY ON THE SEVENTEENTH DAY OF THE TENTH MONTH, IN THE YEAR TWO THOUSAND AND TWENTY-TWO, ELSE THEY WILL BE TOO LATE, AND WE WILL ALL MEET OUR END.

    I KNOW YOU WILL NOT WEEP FOR ME. AFTER ALL, I AM A MORTAL. I DO HOPE, THOUGH, YOU WILL BELIEVE MY NEXT WORDS. FOR ALL THE PAIN I WILL FEEL MOMENTS FROM NOW, IT WILL BE WORTH THE RARE MOMENTS WHEN I SAW YOU SMILE.

    I PRAY THIS MESSAGE FINDS YOU IN TIME.

                                                 - ALES

Chapter One

Elias Riley does not believe in signs from the universe. If he did, he would have to admit that even after twenty-five years of life, he never felt like he was in the right place at all.

"Move it! Coming through!" Two police officers from the Chicago Police Department raced past Eli, sloshing coffee out of the tops of their cups. Eli wrapped his arm around his camera, following behind the officers to the wreckage a block away.

Finally. That was the word playing in his mind when Eli heard the news report about the building fire downtown. Not that he was happy a tragedy had struck, of course. But this was the perfect opportunity for him to finally show his idiot boss, Levi Grimes, what he was capable of. *No more coffee runs and mindless errands for me.*

Three fire trucks blocked off the streets as screams emanated from inside the building. A blaze of red and orange flickered through the building as an enormous cloud of smoke engulfed the entire block. The street became hot enough to melt the ice on the sidewalk, and Eli was sweating inside his winter coat.

Standing on the other side of a firetruck, Eli held up his camera. His excitement grew with every flash as he captured the broken windows, the violent flames, and the devastated faces surrounding him. A slight twinge of guilt pricked at his gut. This was always his least favorite part, feeling like his elation could only come at the cost of others' heartaches. It was a bittersweet storm of emotions and it never quite eased up, no matter how many times he encountered them.

He aimed his camera toward the rubble in the alleyway and froze as he focused his lens on a small girl holding blue-knit blanket. She was crying, staring up at the flames with horror etched on her face. Eli snapped the photo without fully looking into the lens, his eyes glued to the tears glistening on her cheeks.

Where are her parents? The thought had no sooner entered Eli's mind when he heard an explosion overhead. He pushed past the crowd forming outside of the yellow tape, racing toward the child to save her, sure the building would fall on her at any moment.

As he took a step onto the curb, his back foot caught on the edge of the concrete, causing him to face-plant onto the sidewalk with a loud yelp.

Eli picked his head up off the ground in time to see the little girl being escorted away by a firefighter. Glass crunched from underneath him as he lifted himself from the ground. His heart sank as he looked and saw he had landed right on top of his camera, shattering the lens. He groaned in pain and brushed himself off. Grabbing the remains of the camera, he fled the scene before he could embarrass himself further.

Once he was far enough away, he sat on a bench to attempt to pry the camera's memory card out. The card popped out of its slot, unscathed. *At least I still have the photos.* Eli sighed as he watched the story unfold from afar, harboring a familiar feeling of being on the outside looking in.

A vibration came from his coat pocket. As he pulled it out to turn off the alarm, the clock on the screen read 9:07 a.m.

"Shit."

Eli entered the lobby of the Chicago Gazette and rushed toward the elevator. Once inside, he pressed the button for the fifth floor and took a step back, rocking back and forth on his heels in impatience. He fiddled with the memory card in his hand, praying the photos he had gotten would be enough to make up for him being fifteen minutes late again. The doors opened to the fifth floor, and Eli took off down the hallway.

The last time he was late, Levi had screamed at him in front of the entire news staff, whizzing a coffee mug past his head in a rage. Eli hustled up to the editor's office door and knocked, pushing his unkempt brown hair out of his face. The door opened, and Eli arrived face-to-face with Jeanine, Levi's assistant.

"You're late." The older woman said.
"Come on, Jeanine, let me through. I can explain it to him."

She frowned at Eli for a moment before stepping back and opening the door broader for him to enter through. Once he was inside, she nodded to him and stepped out, closing the door behind her, and leaving Eli to his fate. Levi sat behind his desk, looking over a stack of papers, never even glancing up at Eli's arrival.

"Mr. Grimes, I'm so sorry." Eli took a seat in the chair placed at the front of the work surface. "I got the pictures you needed, and I would've been here twenty minutes ago, but—"

"Oh, here we go," Levi looked up from his work and leaned back in his chair. His face was hard and unforgiving as he set his palm on the back of his head and waited for Eli to continue.

"It was crazy downtown." Eli's eyes widened, pleading with his employer to understand. "There were no cabs. The subway stopped. I had to run all the way here."

"Why were you downtown?" Levi asked.

"To get the pictures for the story. The burning building at—"

"Who asked you to do that?"

"Well, no one but—"

"No one did," Levi said, rising from his chair. He was tall and intimidating, and as he talked downward to Eli, his voice grew louder. "Once again, you have taken it upon yourself to create your own job description. You applied as an assistant, and I hired you to assist. To get coffee, to edit, to file—whatever the paper needs. Yet, you constantly do whatever you want to do, and damn everyone else working their asses off in that newsroom out there."

Eli's jaw clenched, and his almond eyes narrowed, looking away from the man looming over him. "I'm not an assistant, Mr. Grimes. I'm a photographer."

"And now you're neither. I'm out of chances for you, Eli. You can go."

"But Mr. Grimes—"

"You're fired." Levi sat back down and returned his attention to the files on his desk. "We will mail your last check to the address on file."

As Eli stepped out of the office and walked down the hallway, stopping outside of the door to the newsroom. Jeanine appeared at his side and lay a hand on his shoulder.

"It's okay to work your way up, you know. It's not a sign of failure." She comforted him.

Eli sighed and turned to face her.

"I appreciate you saying that, but I came here to be a photojournalist. I had a job, a great job—"

"'Had' is the key word there." She interrupted. "Why did you apply for this job, anyway?"

"I wanted to do something more than just take pictures for magazines. I wanted to tell stories, be in the action, and do something that matters. Photojournalism felt like the way to do that." Eli glanced into the newsroom once more, deflated and discouraged.

"But why here? I mean, you're only 25 and you've been published twice. Sure, they weren't popular magazines, but it's still a feat. I read your resume. You could've gone to any press in the country to take photos if it's what you wanted to do."

"I thought maybe, once Levi saw my pictures—"

"What? He'd forget you applied as an assistant?"

"I wanted to come home. After my parents…" Eli swallowed. He shook his head and cleared his throat. "Do you ever feel like there's something more you're supposed to be doing? Like, a reason to make life make any damn sense?"

"I think everyone does, Eli," Jeanine replied. "Some people get lucky and find their calling early. Others search a little longer. It'll come to you when it's meant to."

∎∎

"Aha! Got him!"

Two women sat at a coffee shop patio across from the Gazette, watching as Eli came out of the building and hustled down the steps in front.

"You're sure it's him this time, Artemis?" The older of the two raised a brow. "Not that I don't trust you, but the last one we tried to contact was a four-year-old in Montana."

Artemis wrinkled her nose, "It is not my fault there are eighteen Elias Rileys in the realm, Demeter. I'm a tracker, not a miracle worker."

"As I said, I trust you, dear. I just preferred to be sure."

"Well, I am almost sure. Of that, and also this scone was not worth the four dollars." She grimaced, rising from her seat. "Let's go."

"We need to make entirely sure it's him before we alert the others. Are you sensing anything?"

Artemis closed her eyes and inhaled.

"It's him." She snapped her lids open and looked at Demeter, exhaling. "It's the strongest scent I've ever gotten."

"I would imagine so," Demeter smirked.

"Oh, stop gloating." Artemis shoved her, causing them both to chuckle. "Come on, we've gotta get the message to Hermes!"

Chapter Two

Eli walked the three chilly blocks to his home in Logan Square. Mounds of snow lined the sidewalk, and the concrete was slick under their feet. He recalled a time when he was a kid, and he thought snow came from the filling of a million oatmeal cream pies. A simpler time, Eli thought, shifting his camera bag farther up on his shoulder.

As he rounded the corner onto his street, he looked up toward his home. The cottage somehow looked even colder than he was. At over sixty years old, the house was in good condition, but the upkeep was too much to handle, and it was showing. Eli would have sold it by now. It was a smaller home, but he was alone anyway, and it kept him sheltered and warm. As his fingers numbed, he quickened his pace towards the house.

The inside of his home was as frigid as the outside, making Eli sigh in frustration. He set his cell phone and camera bag down on the counter, and headed straight to the heater, holding his hands to the warmth. Eli closed his eyes for a moment and rubbed his hands together. Once his limbs had thawed out, Eli removed his coat.

He didn't want to think about his broken camera or his newfound unemployment. Instead, he stepped over to a large bookshelf that hugged the length of the far wall. Various knick-knacks and books sat on the shelf and though the novels were old and worn, not a speck of dust was on them. Eli stopped in front of a wedding photo, kissed his fingers, and put them on the frame.

"I'm sorry, mom and dad." He whispered. "I let you both down. Again. I'll do better."

Eli searched the shelves, landing his hands on a thick green book.

"Hello, old friend." He had already read the novel three times, but he took it to the sofa anyway, plopping down on the cushions and opening to the first page. Eli loved re-reading. He hadn't bought a new book in ages. Something was comforting to him about always knowing what was going to happen in the end.

About ten pages in, Eli heard a clatter outside of his front door. He stood up, taking a step backward. The knob twitched, and the door swung open, slamming against the wall with a loud bang. Almost instinctively, Eli dove behind the couch, crouching in silence.

Not again. Not again. Please, not again.

A few moments passed with no sign of noise or danger, making Eli wonder if perhaps it was just the wind that had pushed the door open. But the wind doesn't turn the knob, Eli reminded himself, keeping his guard up. The boy steadied his breathing. He crept to the end of the couch, peeking around the side. As he looked, he saw no one there and breathed a small sigh of relief.

"Who are we hiding from?" A girl's voice whispered from beside him. Eli's heart leaped from his chest as he screamed, jumping away from the girl crouched next to him.

"Who are you?" Eli ran to the front part of the couch as the girl stood as well. "Why did you break into my house?"

"Lucy Stevens, at your service." She gave a sort of half curtsy. "Well, not *your* service, per se. And I had to break in. You locked the door."

She wore a smirk on her heart-shaped face, and she had strawberry blonde hair pulled up into a ponytail that bounced as she spoke. She didn't seem like a criminal, and she was much smaller than him. There was also something oddly comforting about her smile, but Eli remained wary.

"*Why* are you in my house at all?"

"Oh, of course. I'm sorry, I should've led with that." Lucy shook her head. "I've been sent to kidnap you."

"Kidnap me?" Eli's brows furrowed. "Sent by whom?"

"It's 'sent by who'."

"It's really not."

Lucy's gray eyes narrowed. Eli could see the wheels turning before she shook her head and stammered, "Well, either way, you're coming with me. You don't have a choice."

"I'm not going anywhere until you answer my questions, and I don't see you forcing me to do anything." Eli gestured at their obvious size difference.

Lucy smiled. She leaned down, grabbed the underside of the couch, and with no sign of stress, lifted it above her head.

"Do you see it now?" She asked, setting the seat back on all fours. She gave a smug smile, raising her eyebrows at him.

Eli sucked in a gasp. He didn't fully believe his own eyes. The way she lifted the furniture was nothing short of impossible. Eli turned to run, heading back to the front door.

He opened the door about an inch before the handle yanked itself out of his hand and slammed the door shut. He grabbed the knob once more, tugging and pulling, but the door would not budge open. He slowly turned to look at Lucy in disbelief and shock.

"How did—?"
"That's so rude," Lucy sighed. "You shouldn't leave when you have guests."
"Rude? You broke into my house!"
"Tomato, potato."
"Tomato, Tomahto."
"Correct my grammar one more time, and I'll punt you out the door, Egghead."
"Can you at least tell me why you're kidnapping me?"
"It won't be kidnapping if you just come with me."
She rolled her eyes.
"Look, I get you think this is funny, but the last time someone broke into this house…" Eli trailed off, his throat tightening. "This isn't a joke to me. Tell me what you want right now."

Lucy tilted her head, pursing her mouth to the side in thought.

"Fine. You're one of the Five." Lucy offered. "So am I. Even though you have no clue what I'm talking about, there's something in you that wants to come with me. Am I right?"

"One of the Five? What are you talking about?"

Eli felt the urge, though. It was like a calmness washing over him whenever she spoke. Somehow, the sense of peace scared him even more than his actual fear.

"Listen, I know you're scared." Lucy's voice was gentle. "But I wasn't lying."

"About which part?"

"The part where you don't have a choice here."

The strange girl walked past Eli and held her palm up to the entryway. Eli thought he saw a golden light come through the cracks in the door jambs, before disappearing a moment later. Lucy turned to him, winked, and then opened the door wide grabbing Eli's arm. Before he could stop her, she pushed him through the opening and closed the door behind them both.

Chapter Three

Eli's jaw dropped in astonishment. He expected to be thrust back into the frigid Chicago air, but instead, he stood in a large dining area that looked like a 1920s-style speakeasy, packed with beautiful people all dressed in suits and cocktail dresses.

Cigarette smoke permeated the air, creating a haze between Eli and a stage centered at the head of the room. On the wall behind a long wood-topped bar there hung four clocks, each with a different city name underneath. New York, Paris, Tokyo, and Athens. They set each clock to 5 pm, which Eli knew couldn't be accurate.

Chandeliers hung from a pitch-black ceiling, gleaming as if they were mimicking the stars, and each of the tables donned a candlelight votive. On the stage stood a woman, singing a slow jazz tune in a voice almost as gorgeous as she was. Eli struggled to believe what he was seeing. *It has to be a dream. None of this is possible.*

Lucy, still holding his arm, dragged him through the room before stopping at a table near the stage. She sat down and Eli pulled out a chair and plopped into it, placing his elbows on the table and his head in his hands. He rubbed his eyes in the hopes of somehow forcing himself to wake up back in his bed at home.

When he looked at the table once more, a small glass had materialized in front of him. The caramel color inside of it reminded him of whiskey, and the smell was strong enough to reach Eli where he sat. *At least there's alcohol.* He reached for the glass.

"Don't." Lucy smacked his hand away. "You can't eat or drink anything in the Underworld, dummy."

"The Underworld?" Eli snorted. "Now I know I'm dreaming. There's no such thing."

"You sure?"

Eli swallowed hard. "I mean, no one can be sure of anything like that. But it's pretty unlikely, I think."

"Well, unlikely or not, you are currently sitting in The Perished Pub. It's one of the more popular hangouts here in the actual, real, literal, Underworld. And to get it out of the way; Greek Myths are real, you are not dead, and to top it all off," Lucy reached over and pinched Eli's arm, earning her a wince and a glare, "you're not dreaming either."

Eli couldn't help but wonder. It was impossible, but if she were telling the truth, was there a chance his parents- *No.* He pushed the thought from his mind. He had enough heartbreak where they were concerned, he wasn't exactly pumping himself up to go search for more. He refocused on his conversation with Lucy.

"So, you came and shoved me through a mystical door, not even letting me grab my cell phone—"

"It wouldn't have worked here, anyway. Service is terrible."

"Not the point," he continued. "You shoved me through a door into the mythical land of the dead, and I can't even drink here?"

"It's a rough life," she feigned sympathy, "but you'll live, and while you're here, you won't even notice. It's something to do with the magic of this place. You may get a craving for something, but you never feel genuine hunger or thirst."

"That's kind of nice." Eli acknowledged. "But can't I still starve? Just because I don't feel hungry doesn't mean I don't still need food to survive."

"Do you ever do anything other than worry?" Lucy peered at him, cocking her head to the side. "I mean, I've only known you for about thirty minutes and in that time, I've gotten four ulcers just from listening to you talk."

"Milk is good for those," Eli responded.

Lucy rolled her eyes and smirked, looking up at the door. Her eyes lit up, and she began waving at a tall boy who had entered the bar.

"Hey!" The new guy smiled at Lucy as he got closer. "You found Waldo!"

"Who's Waldo?" Eli's brows furrowed.

"No, it's Where's Waldo."

Lucy snorted. "You can ignore Theo. He's been calling you Waldo for months. Like I said earlier, we've been looking for you for a while."

The boy she called Theo took a seat across from them. He was attractive. Not so much in the face, but the energy he was emitting. He had a genuine smile, and Eli felt drawn to him. As if he had known the boy his whole life.

"Okay, now that he's here, can one of you tell me what the hell is happening?" Eli sighed.

Theo snapped his head towards Lucy, his hazel eyes narrowing.

"You didn't tell him anything?" he exclaimed.

"Nope." Lucy grinned.

"Why not?"

"I thought it was funnier."

"Bro—"

Eli interrupted their bickering. "Can someone just explain this to me, please?"

Lucy giggled, reached into her jacket pocket, and pulled out a folded-up piece of paper.

"I think it's easier if we start with this." She handed the paper to Eli. Eli unfolded the paper and read the letter aloud.

"My Dearest Demeter,"

•••

"Am I supposed to know what any of this means?" Eli held up the letter to Theo and Lucy after reading through it. "Who the hell is Ales? Children of Myths? What is this?"

"Like I said before, you're one of the Five," Lucy explained. "The same Five mentioned in that letter who are supposed to save the world. Along with me, Theo, and two others who you'll meet. We are a group of warriors with the blood of five gods and goddesses. From their blood, we got God-like powers so we can fulfill the prophecy and stop the downfall of all life on Earth."

She said it so simply. As if she was just reciting a soup recipe or giving directions to the nearest airport. Eli blinked for a moment, processing what was said, and burst into a fit of laughter.

"Oh, man," He clutched his stomach, "that's the stupidest thing I've ever heard."

"I think he's gone mad," Lucy mumbled to Theo.

"Let's give him a minute," Theo whispered back, smirking.

"Look, I'm sure you guys mean well. Hell, I may even believe you," Eli chuckled, wiping tears from his eyes, "I don't do drugs, so this isn't a trip. I can't read in my dreams, so I'm not asleep. The evidence is leaning towards this being something that is happening."

"Then why the hysterics?" Lucy asked.

"You have the wrong guy," Eli claimed. "I don't have any powers. Trust me, I've wanted to be a hero my whole life, ached for it even. To do something important, to fight all kinds of evils, to matter. That's how I know if you need a warrior, your best bet is to ask anybody else."

Lucy and Theo shared a knowing look between them.

"I'm gonna go call for the car," Lucy slowly rose from the table, nodded at Theo, and left through the front door.

Eli and Theo sat for a moment, Theo fidgeting with a napkin in front of him. Eli would've killed to pound the drink sitting in front of him. 'Overwhelmed' didn't even begin to describe how he was feeling. He yearned for what they were saying to be true but couldn't allow his hopes to rise. He cleared his throat and leaned forward.

"Why me?"

"You know, before they found me," Theo began, ignoring Eli's question, "I was living in Los Angeles, no clue what I was doing. My dad is a film director, and my mom passed when I was in high school, so it was just me and him. Thanks to his job, we were well off, and I never had to worry about having life skills or talents. Life was one big party all the time. I was terrified when I was told I was a 'chosen one'. I went back home, thinking Lucy was just a crazy person."

"Makes sense." Eli couldn't help but chuckle.

"Anyway, the point is, the party had to end. I realized my so-called friends would've sold me for a pack of gum and, as great as my dad was, he was busy all the time. At a certain point, I had nothing left to lose." Theo placed his elbows on the table and leaned his head into his hands. "Bro, I don't have an answer for your questions that's going to make you feel better. You and I were born with a special blood type and that's all there is to it. It just comes down to the luck of the draw. But whether you think something destined you for great things, isn't it enough the universe believes it?"

Eli sighed, understanding all too well the feeling Theo was referencing. A pit formed in his stomach, and he knew his new acquaintance was right. Maybe there was no answer, and maybe everything in life was just the luck of the draw. Just a string of coincidences and happenstances shaping him, yet never helping him. His earlier conversation with Jeanine played on a loop in his mind. If he could make his life mean something, why should it matter why?

Just then, Lucy reappeared, snapping Eli out of his thoughts. She sat back down and turned to face Eli.

"Did you boys have a good talk?"

"Yeah, sort of," Eli answered.

"You are the right guy, Eli," Lucy reassured, "and we can prove it if you'd like?"

Eli fiddled with the tablecloth, thinking. He had no one waiting for him at home, no family left to speak of, and, as of this morning, no job to report back to. *No one would miss me anyway. How pathetic.* He looked up into Lucy's eyes and braced himself.

"Okay then, prove it."

Lucy held out her hand to Eli, and he placed his hand over hers in response. As soon as their palms connected, he felt a heat radiating throughout himself. Shivers ran up his spine and he felt lighter as if he could float away at any moment.

Lucy pulled her hand away and asked, "How do you feel now?"

Incredible. Eli was breathless, his teeth chattering in excitement. Even after her hand was gone, the feeling stayed constant. It was as if electricity was pulsing through his body, lining up in a rhythm with his heartbeat.

"What did you do?"

"I woke you up," Lucy said. "I am the first of the Five. When they found me and awakened my powers, they gifted me the ability to awaken the rest of the Five's powers as well."

"Powers," Eli mused, more to himself than the others.

Theo smiled at him and cleared his throat. "And just so you know, bro, it wouldn't have worked if you were the wrong guy."

This was it, Eli thought to himself. This is what he had been searching for his whole life. Something special, something important. A reprieve from the mundane day-to-day crap everyone else seemed so satisfied with. Eli turned his head and wiped his face, determined that he would not let these strangers see him cry. Another thought occurred to him.

"But wait, it said we have to leave by October 17th. That's in two days."

"Yep," Lucy smirked, "Let's go. We've gotta get you all caught up and meet with the others. gods only know what they've gotten up to."

"I still can't believe we left those two alone together," Theo teased.

"They're not alone, they have a chaperone," Lucy feigned offense.

As the two of them laughed and rose from the table, Eli hesitated.

"Will I ever go home again?"

Lucy and Theo paused. Their faces both showed worry and uncertainty.

"We hope so," Theo replied.

"But for now," Lucy intervened, "there are worse things at stake. Come on, Waldo. We still have to factor in the five minutes you'll spend staring at the sky."

Chapter Four

Lucy was right. Once outside, Eli gazed up at the stars and stood frozen in awe. It was not just a starry night, but a cosmos. Deep blues and purples swirled together to form a backdrop; the stars plotted throughout as if someone spilled white glitter on a multicolored poster board. Eli felt like he could see thousands of galaxies all at once. He almost wondered if it was a painting, but the stars shooting off in all directions answered the question for him.

From the outside, the three-story bar stood wedged in between buildings on a city street. If it weren't for the phenomenon overhead, Eli would think he was back in Chicago, or even in New York. A long black Town car sat parked at the front of the establishment, and Lucy and Theo guided Eli over to it. The three piled into the backseat. But Eli couldn't help but notice there was no one in the driver's seat.

"Are we waiting for someone else?"
"No?" Theo said, puzzled. "Should we be?"
"Who's driving then?"
"Oh, yeah, the cars drive themselves here. No one wants to live out their deaths dealing with road rage, you

know?”

“Is that even safe?” Eli asked.

“You're in the Underworld. Are you concerned about a fender bender?” Lucy teased.

“When you put it that way, I guess not,” Eli responded, lost in thought. “But on that note, what happens to us if we get hurt here? Since we're still living and all.”

“Nothing at all. While we're here, we get treated like the locals. You could smoke, drink, or even jump from a roof. You'll find yourself still healthy and all in one piece.” Theo explained.

“Incredible,” Eli moved to grab his seatbelt out of reflex before comprehending what Theo had just said. He put it back, his face hot as he saw the two trying to hide their chuckling.

“You'll get used to it,” Theo assured him.

Eli watched out the window as the buildings raced past them. Five minutes later, the car pulled to a stop, and a robotic voice announced from the front seat, 'You have arrived at your destination.'

“A hotel?”

“Not just any hotel. The Netherworld Express. This place was rated five stars in the Dead Guide. It's where we're staying.” Theo explained.

“Okay, why wasn't I brought here then? Why bother with the bar?”

“There are only three ways into the Underworld, Waldo.” Lucy began. “You fly, you die, or you portal. From what I know, you can't fly, so unless you wanted me to kill you, a portal was the only option.”

“And you can't portal to the hotel?”

“You can portal out of the Underworld using any door but getting back requires you to come in through the pub entrance. It's the best way to keep track of anyone coming and going."

The trio exited the vehicle and stood in front of a grand hotel. Looking upwards, Eli could not even find where the hotel ended, and the sky began. He followed behind Lucy as they made their way inside to the main lobby and then took a left to the elevators. Theo pressed the Penthouse button, and the three piled inside once the doors opened. Eli did not even feel the elevator move before the doors opened once more, an impossibility that he was unable, or just too tired, to fathom.

When the doors opened, they revealed the most stunning hotel room Eli had ever seen. The furniture was modern and luxurious. There were two sitting areas, a dining room, and a kitchen, all in the main room alone. Along the wall to his left were five doors, and along the back was a wall of windows. Eli stepped further into the penthouse, taking in the magnitude of his surroundings. He walked over to the windows and sucked his breath in at the view.

He was starting to believe that Lucy was incapable of saying something wrong, now feeling a little faint himself. It was a panorama of colors, both light, and dark, and in front of them was a giant black castle. Lucy walked over and joined him.

"What is that?" He motioned to what looked like a luminous blue river but was floating like a winding staircase from the sky to the ground. It landed in a large body of water as it reached the bottom, creating a moat around the castle.

"That's Acheron." Lucy informed, "It's one of the five rivers of the Underworld. That's the river that Charon uses to ferry the souls of the living."

"And the castle?"

"We call it the HOH or House of Hades. He doesn't call it that though, so don't say it around him, trust me."

"Trust you? You've met Hades? That's his house?"

"Yes, yes, and yes. He's a nice guy, but very particular. I guess you don't get to be King of the Underworld without being a little strict, though."

Eli stared, agape, at the notion that this was all real. Hades, the Underworld, Greek Myths.

"Careful," Lucy teased. "If your mouth opens any wider, you may drool."

"To be fair, this is all pretty amazing." Eli countered. He paused for a moment. "I thought this place would be sadder, though. More brimstone and fire, I guess."

"You're thinking of Tartarus. That's where the wicked souls go," Lucy pointed over to their left and Eli saw in the distance a bright and roaring fire, a sight that made him queasy just from looking at it. She then pointed to their right. "And over there is Elysium, where only the best souls go."

Eli teared up when he saw the bright white light illuminating the vast green hills. It was as if it was inside of a giant bubble that somehow shielded it from the darkness that surrounded it.

"We're in Netherworld Square. It's kind of in the middle of places. Hades got bored a few decades ago and decided his palace would overlook a city with bustling crowds. No jobs unless you want to work. Just people with true free will, living how they never could on earth."

"Wouldn't that make this the best place, then?" Eli asked her.

"You would think. But with the pleasures of life, they also lose their chance at knowing peace. In Elysium, there's no thinking. No wondering, no worrying. Here, every day is the same. You can never rest. If you ask me, it's the worst place."

"Hm."

"Oh, also, check out that hill over there." Eli looked at where she was pointing. There was an enormous mountain off to the right of Tartarus, made of stone with a cliff at the top.

"It looks like any other hill I've seen. What's so special about it?"

"Have you ever heard the story of Sisyphus?"

Eli shook his head in response.

"Well, he was a mortal man who cheated death twice," Lucy explained. "Ares caught him the first time. After he finally died a third time, Zeus decreed he would punish him by forcing him to push a boulder up a hill for the rest of eternity. That's the hill."

Eli felt his jaw opening wider as she spoke. These were mere fairytales moments before, and it was difficult for him to wrap his mind around the fact that it was all real. He walked to one couch and sat, attempting to calm himself. Eli found it hard to convince himself to look around anymore, overwhelmed by all the emotions coursing through him.

Lucy strode over and plopped herself down next to Eli, while Theo went to the third door on the wall. He knocked twice, and the door opened. A tall guy, who looked about the same age as Eli, strode out of it. The boy looked annoyed at the interruption, or maybe that was just his face. Eli couldn't make out what was being said, but after what seemed like much effort on Theo's part, both boys walked into the living area as well and joined them.

"Eli, this is Wyatt," Theo introduced the boy, as they both had a seat on the lounge across from Eli and Lucy. "Wyatt, Eli."

Wyatt nodded his greeting. Eli didn't get the same feeling from Wyatt that he had gotten from Theo. No warmth or friendliness was coming from the boy. He was acting more so like Eli was intruding somehow.

Eli nodded back, "Hello."

"Where's Liv?" Lucy asked.

"How should I know?" Wyatt narrowed his eyes at her, a slight twang in his voice "I haven't seen her since she left with Dionysus earlier."

"That explains why you're so pouty." She frowned, earning her a sharp glare.

"Oh, shut up, orphan Annie."

"Make me, Poindexter."

"Children please, not in front of Waldo." Theo rolled his eyes, smirking.

"Wait," Eli's eyes grew large, "Dionysus? The real Dionysus? The Greek god of wine?"

"Can I go back to my room now?" Wyatt asked before turning back to Eli. "Like, no offense, great to meet you, but I'm really just not in the mood to walk a toddler through calculus right now."

"What the hell is that supposed to mean?"

"Do you really need me?" Wyatt asked Theo again, ignoring Eli's question completely.

"Fine," Theo sighed. "Just go."

Wyatt grinned and made his way back inside the room he came from. He reminded Eli of Jack Torres, an awful kid that used to bully him in middle school. Between the temper, the arrogance, and the blond crew-cut hair, the resemblance was uncanny.

"What's his deal?" Eli asked.

"He's better once you get to know him," Theo said.

"Debatable," Lucy rolled her eyes. "He keeps to himself a lot, when he's not with Liv, of course. But he's a grade a know-it-all."

"Oh, so he and Liv are dating?"

"Most days, if you wanna call it that." Her eyebrows waggled.

Eli let out a snort at the gesture.

"Lucy is making him sound a lot worse than he is." Theo frowned.

"The reason we have god-like powers," Lucy ignored him, "is because we're long descended from the gods themselves. My blood comes from Hermes, Theo's comes from Dionysus, Liv's comes from Aphrodite."

"Okay, but what does that have to do with Wyatt?" Eli asked.

"Well," Lucy explained, "Wyatt's blood comes from Apollo."

"Okay?"

"Ugh," she sighed, "have you just read none of the lore?"

"Let's pretend I haven't."

"Ooh, I love playing pretend," she simpered.

Eli's face flushed as Lucy smirked at him.

"Anyway," she continued, "Apollo has some issues with being possessive, knowing everything, and he has a bit of a God complex, pun intended. So, Wyatt likes to think he's the leader of the pack as if we even need one."

"So, when he said he didn't have time to 'teach a toddler calculus'…"

"Oh, he was calling you stupid, for sure."

"He didn't mean it in a bad way," Theo defended.

"You just got here, so there's a lot you don't know."

"Still sucks to hear, though," Eli thought aloud, "and when you said he was pouty, about Dionysus, is that because he's jealous or something?"

"See, he's catching on," Lucy smirked at Theo.

"Isn't Dionysus older than all of us? Wait, how old are you guys?"

"We're all twenty-five, same as you," Theo answered.

"So, like, *way* older than all of us then."

"Yeah, but the gods choose the age they look." Theo chuckled. "I'm pretty sure he wouldn't actually do anything with Liv, though."

"Wouldn't you?" Lucy challenged, "I mean, even I would. That girl is gorgeous."

Eli raised his eyebrows.

"Aw, don't worry, Waldo. You're cute too." She inched closer to him, her lip curling.

Eli's face turned red and felt hot. "Oh, uh- I wasn't-," he cleared his throat and shifted in his seat.

Lucy burst into laughter. "I like you better when you're flustered."

"Hey, guys, I'm right here," Theo broke the tension, "and we still have to bring Waldo up to speed so, let's do that instead of whatever the hell this was."

"Wait," Eli felt discombobulated, but he managed to form the words. "Who does my blood come from?"

"Demeter," Theo answered, "she's the nicest. You'll like her."

Eli inhaled, unsure. He was no stranger to being let down. He had no family left to speak of and felt there was no point in getting excited over familial bonding, especially when he would probably never see any of these people after this. He segued back to the conversation prior.

"Okay, so, get me up to speed, then."

Theo cleared his throat and sat forward.

"So, you read the letter and know you're descended from Demeter, and a member of the Five, the last member we had to find. Lucy was the first member found about a year ago, then me and Wyatt. Liv was the most recent until you got here. We found her about 6 months ago. Tomorrow, you'll have some one-on-one training time with Demeter so you can figure out your powers. In two days, we start on our journey to the Isle of Extinction. Once there, we forge the weapon, kill the bad guy, and save the world," Theo grinned, pumping his fist in the air.

"That easy, huh?" Eli said, amused.
"Eh, maybe with some ups and downs mixed in there somewhere. Questions so far?"
"Only about a million." He responded. "For instance, if they started looking for us a year ago, why was I so hard to find?"
"I don't know that one." Theo frowned. "Artemis, the goddess, was the one who tracked us all down. She actually started tracking us decades ago but had to wait until we were older to know for sure and approach us. I know some of us were easier to find because of our lifestyles and notoriety, but there aren't that many Elias Rileys in the world. I would've thought you would be the first one found. Maybe you can ask Demeter."

"Okay." Eli agreed, saving that thought for later. "Next question. Why now? How did they know when this was going to happen? A year wasn't exactly stated in the letter."
"Wyatt actually has a theory it's because of our age." Theo offered. "We're all twenty-five so it's five times five, ya know? But none of the gods will tell us that one. They

don't necessarily hide things from us, but we are on a need-to-know basis."

"What wouldn't we need to know? If our situation is so life-and-death, why wouldn't they tell us everything?"

Theo pursed his lips in thought. "While we're the ones who actually have to fight, we're still just mortals, children in their eyes. They're the actual gods, so they pick and choose the knowledge they give away."

"Okay, and speaking of fighting," Eli said, "who exactly is this mighty god we're supposed to be defeating?"

"Ooh, ooh, don't worry Theo, I'll take the easy one." Lucy piped up, grinning. "We're gonna kill Zeus."

■■■

"Nope."

Eli rose from the couch and headed back towards the elevator.

"Where are you even trying to go?" Theo followed behind. "You're in the Underworld, remember?"

Lucy remained seated, a look of boredom on her face. Eli understood she had been dealing with this for a year, but her indifference to his reaction made him angry. As if he was merely overreacting to this very impossible and very terrifying task. The look on her face made him feel like a child, being told he was just being dramatic after falling off the swing set. Just because someone else had been through it before, didn't make it hurt any less.

Where would he even go, though? Even if he could leave the hotel, and escape the Underworld, what was he going back to? That was his thought earlier too, he recalled feeling more pathetic than he ever had before.

"Most days I'm sure I have nothing to live for," his words came out strained, "but that doesn't mean I'm ready to die."

Eli's throat tightened at the realization that it was the most honest thing he had ever said to another person.

Theo placed his arm around Eli's shoulders, guiding him back to the couch.

"I know it sucks, bro," he sympathized, "but you've got us now, and the prophecy literally says we're gonna win."

"You just said it yourself, Theo." Eli plopped back down on the couch. "I'm already behind. In two days, we have to go on a journey to defeat the most powerful god in all of Greek mythology. How am I going to do that?"

"You have powers, remember?" Lucy's voice was gentle but rehearsed. "After training tomorrow, after you see what you can do, you'll feel better about it, I promise."

Eli relaxed, but not by much. "What are we even stopping Zeus from doing? I know the prophecy mentioned pride and greed, but what is he attempting here?"

Theo and Lucy glanced at each other again.

"Would you guys knock it off?" Eli's eyes narrowed. "Stop it with the knowing glances and the kid gloves. If you expect me to fight with you, treat me like it."

"That's fair." Theo agreed. "Zeus is planning on mass extinction."

Eli felt his breath catch, terror washing over him.

"According to Demeter," Lucy took over, "he's decided that he liked it better in the olden days when everyone worshiped the gods on Mount Olympus. He's been plotting for decades now to do away with all humankind. To start from scratch and be the one True God amongst the false idols."

"That's insane." Eli swallowed hard.

"Which is where we come in," Theo emphasized. "We've got the means to stop him, and we're gonna."

Lucy placed her hand on Eli's. "I get that you're scared. But we can fight and maybe win or do nothing and die for sure."

"Well, when you put it like that," Eli sighed, but the perspective helped. He was still terrified, but what was there to be done?

"Come on, Waldo," Theo smiled, heading to the fifth door down, "I'll show you to your room."

"Nighty night, boys," Lucy giggled as she sauntered away and disappeared into the first door on the wall. Eli followed Theo through the second door.

Chapter Five

"This is my room?"

The size of the room was twice the size of his entire living room back home. Eli couldn't even wonder how it fits within the rest of the penthouse, as large as it was. The walls were Eli's favorite shade of light blue. A king-sized bed sat against the center of the wall, and there was a long couch on the opposite side. Eli had never slept in a king-sized bed before. He walked over and flopped down on it, stretching his arms out wide and inhaling fresh laundry soap. He laughed despite himself and sat up straight. Theo watched him with a grin, leaning against the door frame.

"There's another door over there," Theo nodded to the back of the room, "that's your bathroom, and there are towels and anything else you might need in the closet on the left when you first walk in. If you need anything else, I'm in door two."

Eli stopped him. "I have another question."

"Shoot."

"So," he began, thinking how best to word what he wanted to say, "I know that you've all been here way longer than me but, how—"

"Are we all so chill about what's going on?" Theo finished his thought. Eli nodded in response.

"I'm a pretty chill person anyway," he began, "but we all had the same first reaction you did, pretty much. I don't know for sure about Lucy since she was here before me. But Wyatt was similar, and Liv was way worse."

"Really?" Eli felt a little better, less alone.

"Yeah, she was emotional about leaving her family and her job."

"What was her job?" Eli's curiosity peaked. It wasn't often that he heard someone was sad about not having to work.

"She's a pretty successful model. Makes sense, with her being the descendent of Aphrodite and all. It's funny, we had actually met at a few events when she worked in L.A. I think that's why it was so easy to find the both of us."

"Oh wow, small world." Eli mused. "But if they found you both at the same time, then why was she fourth?"

"She was much harder to get to than I was," Theo laughed. "She had three bodyguards that never let her out of their sight, so Lucy could never get her alone. Aphrodite had to go herself to retrieve Liv. She masqueraded as one of the other models at LA Fashion week."

"Makes sense." Eli wondered why Lucy, herself, didn't just pretend to be the model. He doubted anyone would have questioned her.

"Oh, before I forget," Theo snapped his fingers. "When I moved in, I was worried mostly about my dad, but they let me send him a letter, just letting him know I was okay. They can do that for you too if you need to?"

"Nah," Eli answered honestly, "I don't have anyone who would miss me."

"Do you want to talk about it?" Theo tilted his head.

Eli sat in silence for a moment, realizing that he did. He took a deep breath.

"My parents were killed. I was 17 and someone broke in—" Eli's voice shook. "I don't remember that much, just my mom telling me to stay in my room, and then the gunshots."

"Holy shit." Theo exhaled. "I'm so sorry. I don't even know what to say."

"That's fine. I'm sure you know, because of your mom, there really isn't a right thing *to* say."

"True." Theo looked down at his shoes.

"Anyway," Eli ventured, desperately wanting to change the subject, yet already regretting his next words, "Lucy seems...nice."

"She's not," Theo chuckled. "Like, she's a good person, but you have to develop a thick skin with her. I think she uses humor as a coping mechanism."

"Coping from what, do you know?"

"No clue. The most I've gathered from Dionysus is that her home life wasn't great. She was a foster kid, I guess."

Eli shifted uncomfortably, wishing he hadn't asked. He felt weird, wrong even, to be talking about this with Theo.

"Be careful, if you're thinking about her like *that*," Theo warned.

"I don't even know how I could think about anyone like that at a time like *this*."

"You're still human," Theo smirked. "But, going back to your first question, Lucy was right about your powers. Once you get into training tomorrow and see what you can do, it'll be way easier to come to terms with what has to be done. And even though some of us may not be as friendly as others, we've got each other's backs."

"Thanks," Eli smiled at him.

"No problem." He replied. He turned to leave, and called over his shoulder, "Sweet dreams, Waldo."

Eli's eyes began feeling heavy, and with a yawn, he felt how tired he was for the first time since arriving. A tall, antique dresser sat beside the door. Inside, Eli found a pair of black pajamas in his exact size and noticed there were more clothes as well. He breathed a sigh of relief that he wouldn't have to continue wearing the same outfit the entire journey.

As he got into bed, he was concerned that he would have trouble sleeping. So many things had happened in such a brief period, he didn't imagine his brain could find any peace from that. But, as soon as he laid his head down on a pillow as soft as a marshmallow, all of his worries disappeared, and he fell asleep.

• •

Crash

Eli was startled awake and sat up. The noise had been loud, and it came from right outside his door. He took a few cautionary steps towards it, grabbing the knob quietly and creaking the door open slowly. As light came through the cracks, he heard a giggle and was sure it was not Lucy's. Not that he had it memorized, or anything, he assured himself. He peeked his head outside and saw two figures in the kitchen.

One figure he assumed was Liv, just from the description 'blood of Aphrodite.' The girl was tall, blonde, and beautiful, with an oval face and a button nose. There was also an attractive man standing at her side. He looked older than Eli but not by much, maybe late-20's if he had to guess.

The pair were shushing each other, and moving a pan as quietly as possible, which was the exact moment Eli realized they were both tipsy. He tried to creep back inside and close the door, but the woman spotted him too quickly.

"Oh, my gods, are you Eli?" She gleamed, "Come out, come out! I have *so* been looking forward to meeting you!"

Eli opened the door wider and shuffled into the kitchen with them.

"You're cute, too." She noted once he got closer, and turned to the man to ask, "How is it we just so happen to be the most attractive Five there's ever been?"
"Just luck, I guess." The man responded. "Also, you're the only Five that's ever been."
"Sorry, I didn't mean to interrupt anything," Eli started.
"Not at all," the man assured, "This is Olivia, and my name is Dionysus."

Eli grabbed a hold of the edge of the counter to stop himself from falling over.

"Oh, hello, uh, sir?" No, that didn't feel right. "Excellency? Godliness?"
"It's fine. You can call me Dionysus." The god snickered.

Liv brushed past Dionysus and wrapped Eli in a hug, squeezing hard despite Eli keeping his hands to his sides.

"I am just so happy that you are finally here." She let go of him and walked back to where she was standing previously. The affected way she spoke simultaneously charmed and annoyed Eli. It was as if she needed to enunciate every word perfectly and clearly. "But I am so sorry we woke you up. I'm sure you've had a long day, what with leaving your girlfriend behind to go fight a mighty god and all."
"Oh, I don't have a girlfriend."

"Boyfriend, then?" she prodded, tilting her head to the side.

"No?"

"He said no with a question mark, did you hear it?" Liv asked Dionysus.

"I did. Perhaps there's some confusion on his end."

"Perhaps, indeed."

"Nope." Eli found himself amused at their interaction. "No confusion here."

"Well, *that* is good to know." Liv was incredibly flirtatious; way more than Lucy had been earlier.

"I'm more confused, though," Eli attempted to redirect the conversation, "because it seems like you've had, um…"

"A few drinks?"

"Yeah, exactly. But I thought we couldn't drink anything down here?"

"We can't," Liv explained. "Dionysus took me to the most beautiful restaurant in Santorini. We had drinks there."

"I was just making sure Olivia made it in safely. Until she decided she wanted brownies, that is." Dionysus glanced over at Eli. "Which, as you've stated, she can't have here. Thus, the game of keeping the pan away began."

"Ooh, thanks for reminding me!" Liv exclaimed as she dove back into the pantry. Dionysus rolled his eyes and started after her.

As the two bickered playfully, Eli noticed movement out of the corner of his eye. He looked over to see Wyatt's blonde head pop out of the opening into his room, trying to find the source of all the commotion. Wyatt watched the pair with a look of sadness and irritation before he retreated inside his room. Eli couldn't help but feel sorry for the guy. As much of a jerk as he was, it must suck to see someone you like with someone else.

"Fine." Liv's exaggerated sigh brought Eli back to the moment. "No brownies for me, then."

"Thank you," Dionysus exhaled in relief.

"Are you at least gonna come tuck me in?" She pouted to him.

The god ruffled her bangs, took a step back, and replied, "Get some sleep, kid."

Liv's shoulders slumped in disappointment, but she didn't ask again. Eli also noted that instead of going into the fourth door, she flounced, instead, into Wyatt's room. Eli shook his head in disbelief, and Dionysus looked over at him and smiled.

"She's a handful, huh?" He chuckled. "Now, you get back to bed, too. You've got a big day tomorrow, Elias."

"Nice meeting you, sir." Eli nodded to the god and went back to his room, falling into bed, and drifting off once more.

■ ■

"That Olivia will be the death of me, Apollo." Dionysus plopped onto the large couch in his suite. "Why do we have to stay here again? And why didn't we get to stay in the penthouse? It feels a little unfair, to be honest."

Apollo put down his bow that he had been polishing, rolling his eyes at his brother.

"We're staying here," Apollo said, "because those five warriors are risking their lives for ours. And they're getting the penthouse for the same reason. Perhaps, if you were thinking more clearly with the correct head, you wouldn't be whining so much."

"But you've seen her, brother! It's hardly my fault that she's so beautiful."

"That mindset is almost as ancient as you are, Dionysus." Apollo glared. "We all know better by now than to blame the women for our urges."

"That is not what I meant, and you know it, Apollo. Plus, it was never me who had that issue, was it?" Dionysus sat up, squinting at his brother, angrily.

A tall woman with long blonde hair strode into the room. She yawned and rubbed her dazzling green eyes, squinting at the light.

"Boys, please." She stepped over to them, a frown on her face. "Must you always bicker like this? Some of us are trying to sleep."

"Sorry, Aphrodite," Dionysus sighed.

"Yes, sister, our deepest apologies," Apollo smirked and picked up his bow and rag once more. "Perhaps you could talk some sense into the god trying to sleep with your descendent. Since my doing it is keeping you from your precious beauty sleep."

"The god trying to do what?" The goddesses growled.

Apollo laughed as she chased Dionysus around the room, grabbing potted plants from the end tables to chuck at his head.

"I wasn't gonna do it, Aph! He's making it up, I swear! Ow, please, not the cactus!"

Aphrodite threw the prickly plant directly at her brother's head. Just before the terracotta smashed into Dionysus, another man materialized, snatching it out of the air.

Dionysus stayed cowering, his hands in front of his face, slowly opening one eye. Once he saw he was no longer in danger, he stood up straight and grinned.

"Hey, thanks, Hermes. She just went psycho for no reason. It was insane."

"Dionysus, please shut up." Hermes set the cactus down on one of the end tables. "I wouldn't have to be here to know it was your fault, somehow."

Dionysus rolled his eyes, taking a seat on the couch once more and grumbling, "Well, that's just rude."

Hermes grabbed a seat on the chair across from him, gesturing to the others to do the same. Sharing a look of confusion, Apollo and Aphrodite followed suit. Once they were all sitting, Hermes pulled out a scroll, placing it on the coffee table in between the four of them. He cleared his throat and rolled it open.

"Zeus' latest decree," Hermes announced.

The others read, their faces twisting into anger and shock as their eyes roamed further down the paper.

"He can't do that." Aphrodite's eyes welled up with tears.

"He just did." Apollo sat back against the couch; fury written on his face.

'As the King god of Mount Olympus, I hereby decree that any god or goddess caught assisting the group of warriors, also known as The Five, are to be arrested on sight for treason. They are to be thrown into Tartarus with no opportunity to stand Trial. This Law goes into effect immediately, and with no mercy.'

"How is Elias settling in, Dionysus?" Apollo asked. "You just saw him, right? Does he look like he'll be able to do his training in time?"

"He seemed like a nice kid, I guess," Dionysus shrugged. "I only spoke to him for a few minutes. He's very nervous, though. Something tells me he had some anxiety before Lucy even showed up."

"Oh, well, that's just great." Aphrodite rolled her eyes.

"Don't fret, sister," Hermes comforted her. "Demeter is his trainer. She'll make sure he's ready."

"I just can't believe Zeus could really kill his own family." Dionysus shuddered, focusing their attention back on the scroll. "He can't get to us here, though, right? This only affects the upper realms?"

Apollo smiled wryly, "I guess staying in the Underworld doesn't seem so bad after all. Does it, brother?"

Chapter Six

"We seriously don't have time for coffee?"

Eli and Theo arrived outside the arena just before 9 am, or so Eli was told. With no sun in the sky and no phone to check the time, he just had to assume Theo was telling him the truth, no matter how heavy his eyes still felt.

"Nah, we did." Theo closed the car door and tossed Eli a bottle of water. "But you're gonna need to be hydrated for this."

Eli groaned, loosening the cap.

"Wait." He stopped himself just before taking a swig. "I can't drink this here."

"Water's the only heavenly exception. You can have water anywhere." Theo stated. "That would be like saying that if sweat falls off your face and into your mouth, boom! You're just stuck here forever. That wouldn't be fair at all."

"I guess." Eli looked into the bottle, still feeling unsure. "I'm gonna take your word for it, but if I end up trapped here, I'm trapping you with me."

Theo chuckled as Eli drank, both boys heading into the arena.

Even though the night sky still swirled overhead, and there were no stadium lights around, Eli could see everything in the Underworld Colosseum perfectly. The arena reminded him of the ancient gladiator fights pictured in his history books at school. Columns lined the stadium, and there were rows upon rows of seats made of stone, enough to seat thousands.

Eli had never been very athletic. His mom had enrolled him in sports as a kid, but he had always preferred his books and camera over being pummeled for a football. Looking around the enormous arena now, he couldn't help but wonder what he had missed out on. There was a certain type of energy flowing through the air, the smell of fresh-cut grass filling Eli's senses. Something about the wide, open field made Eli want to do a cartwheel as if he was nothing more than a child.

Theo led him to the front of the track, where they found an older woman waiting. She wore a long green dress and had graying brown hair that fell to her waist. Her eyes squinted at the edges as if they were crinkled in permanent amusement, and her smile was bright.

"Theodore, Elias." The woman welcomed them. "I'm so glad you made it. Traffic wasn't too bad, I hope."
"Oh, it was the worst." Theo teased. "As always."

The woman laughed at Theo's reply before turning to Eli.

"Elias, it is so wonderful to meet you, finally." Her brown eyes gleamed. "My name is Demeter. I am your ancestor and your trainer for the day."

Eli had known that he was coming to meet her, but actually being in her presence stunned him into silence. He stared at her, his eyes wide. In a moment of panic, he bowed at the waist.

Demeter smiled and shot a look at Theo, who chuckled and nudged Eli, shaking him from his stupor.

Eli stood up straight and cleared his throat. "He-hello. Nice to meet you as well, ma'am."

"There we go. That's much better." Demeter acknowledged, "Now, we really must get started. Are you staying to watch, Theodore?"

"Nah," Theo shook his head, "Apollo and Dionysus have us group training this morning. I'll be back with everyone else in a few hours."

"Should Elias not be a part of the group training?" She inquired.

"I thought so too, but Dionysus said his solo training is more important. He said that he'd send you a message."

Demeter frowned but nodded. "Okay, thank you Theodore."

"Wait, you're leaving?" Eli shot Theo a scared look.

"I'll be back soon." He promised. "Good luck, Waldo."

"Never heard of it," Eli mumbled.

Theo patted him on the shoulder and gave a small wave to Demeter before parting, leaving only Eli and the goddess alone in the vast stadium.

"Okay then, shall we?" Demeter guided Eli over into the grass and sat on a bench, gesturing for him to have a seat next to her. "So, tell me about yourself, Elias. How are you feeling about everything so far?"

"What? Oh, I'm fine." Eli said curtly, trying to be as polite as possible while also hating what was happening.

All he wanted to do was get on with the training. He hadn't expected some sort of heart-to-heart, or whatever this was. The goddess must have sensed his reserve.

"It seems as though you dislike me," she began, slowly, "yet you do not know me. Have I done something wrong in the five minutes since you arrived?"

"No, not at all," he replied respectfully. "It's just that we really don't have to do this."

Demeter raised an eyebrow at him. "Do what? The training?"

"No, the talking. Like, getting to know each other, family bonding stuff. With all due respect, we're not family just because I'm your descendant. I already had a family, and it didn't work out so great. I'm not really up for more of that, you know?"

"I see." She nodded understandingly. "Well, why don't you tell me about your actual family, then?"

"Are you a goddess or a therapist?"

"I am whatever you might need me to be, dear." Demeter placed her hand on his arm, and he felt a warmth spread throughout his body.

Before Eli understood what was happening, he was telling her everything, the words coming out as involuntarily as throwing up. He explained his parents' deaths, the loss that he carried with him to this day, and his unrelenting need to find a way to make them proud. He even told her he felt like a fool because all he ever wanted was to be a hero, special, and now that he was here, he was terrified. Once he had finished, he became angry.

"What did you do?" His eyes flashed.

"I simply helped," she said, sweetly.

"Helped?" Eli exclaimed. "You just forced me to tell you my entire life story. What is the matter with you?"

"First of all," Demeter's tone grew assertive, reminding Eli just who he was speaking to, "when I put my hand on you, all I did was calm your inner mind. I did not coerce you into telling me anything. Only once you were comfortable enough, healed enough from the demons in your mind, did you trust me enough to tell me how you were truly feeling."

Eli felt guilty, and a little scared. He stood by the fact that he had no way of knowing that it wasn't a form of mind control. Well, to himself, anyway.

"Second," her smile returned, "thank you ever so much for asking what the matter with me is. I have recently grown concerned about a flock of crows that have been terrorizing the radishes that grow near my home. Now, the scarecrow was completely useless, so I'm thinking about leaving food for the crows somewhere else, so they'll go there instead."

Eli tentatively smiled. "You could always put them in a greenhouse."
"The crows? No, that would be inhumane, I think."
"No," Eli laughed. "The radishes, so that the crows couldn't get to them."
"My dear boy, I'm the goddess of the harvest. I've been doing this for eons. Greenhouses are new-age nonsense."
"Yeah, but it would solve your crow problem, and then you'd be able to grow your crops in the winter, too." His voice trailed off.

It finally clicked in Eli's mind that if Demeter truly existed, Persephone would too. Since her going to the Underworld was the only reason for winter, he feared he would upset Demeter by bringing it up.

"In the winter, you say?" Demeter's eyes widened.
"I'm sorry, I didn't mean to—"

"Not at all," she said kindly. "That sounds lovely. I never realized they were capable of such things. I often look for ways to spend my time while my daughter is away."

"Would she be here now?" Eli inquired, "It was the start of winter when I got pulled here."

"She is, in fact. I wish you could meet her," Demeter frowned. "Unfortunately, I don't believe she'll have the time. Persephone and her husband stay terribly busy."

"I imagine so. Are you, at least, going to get to see her?"

"Sweet boy. I actually just came from her home before meeting you here."

"Good," Eli replied. "It's important to spend time with family, I hear."

"Indeed, it is." Demeter grinned.

She stood up and walked a few steps before stopping to kneel where a wooden crate sat. She opened the top and revealed various weaponry.

"These are all weapons of the gods. The gods themselves have used all of them, and a few of them are even older than I am."

There were bows, swords, and even a mace, from what Eli could tell. One weapon stood out above them all, though he couldn't see what it was, just the shine of its golden handle. He stood as well, moving closer to get a better look. As if reading his mind, Demeter grabbed that very weapon and stood up, presenting it to him.

"Have you heard of the story of Heracles and the Hydra?" Demeter asked.

"Do you mean Hercules?"

"That cartoon, I swear." She wrinkled her nose. "Terribly inaccurate. It's made Charon's job so much harder, as well. Thanks to the portrayal, everyone thinks the Underworld is the Greek version of hell, so they just automatically start arguing with the ferryman that they don't deserve to go there, not realizing that it's the only way to get to Elysium."

Eli was momentarily amused at the thought of a scary underworld God having to argue with people all day. As if he was simply working a customer service job instead of ferrying the dead.

"I imagine that's frustrating." He concealed his smirk. "I think I know the story, though. The Hydra was the monster who grew two heads when you sliced off one, right?"
"Exactly, and this is the sword that Heracles used to kill it."

Eli's eyes widened. As he accepted the weapon from the goddess, he got a closer look. He realized it was also a sword, but that not only the handle was gold, but the entire blade was also. The hilt had etchings reminiscent of the battle Demeter had just spoken of, showing a mighty hero vanquishing the terrible beast, cutting himself out of its stomach.

"How does that feel?" the goddess inquired. "Good? Bad?"
"It's uh, it's fine," Eli replied, holding back his thoughts so as not to look foolish.

Holding the weapon felt like a breath of fresh air. It was as if the sword was a long-lost friend he was finally seeing after decades apart. Eli could feel energy seeping off of it and into himself, charging some mystical battery inside of him.
"Just fine?" She raised an eyebrow, confirming to Eli

that she could see right through his façade.

Eli exhaled. "It's fantastic. It's so sharp, too."

"The beauty about our weapons is they will never dull. They're magically imbued with the power of the ones who wield them, and the strength of any beasts that they defeat."

"Well, this one feels pretty damn powerful."

"Good." Demeter laughed, pulling another sword from the chest. "Now, let's make sure you can use it."

■■

Eli was sure that he was dead as he lay on the cold grass, staring up at the cosmos. He closed his eyes and took a couple of slow breaths.

"How long have I been this out of shape?" he wondered aloud, croaking out the question. He and Demeter had only been sparring for an hour, and his entire body was aching all over.

"Need a hand?" He heard Demeter's voice from above where he lay.

"I'm a goner." Eli gave an exaggerated sigh. "Just leave me here to die."

"I see." the goddess responded, playfully. "Alright then, any last words before I go?"

"Tell Theo he's awesome. Tell Wyatt he's an ass."

Demeter cackled, "Come now, Elias, *those* are your last words?"

Eli chuckled as well, wincing at his aching insides. Demeter leaned down and placed a hand on his chest. After a moment, the boy felt the same warmth from earlier spread throughout him, and his pains completely disappeared.

"Whoa, thanks," He exclaimed, sitting up straight.

"How'd you do that?"

"All a part of my special skill set. And now that you're up, we can work on yours."

Demeter helped the boy to his feet and eyed him up and down. Eli felt uncomfortable with the way she was looking at him. No, not necessarily at him. She seemed to look for something, and after a moment, she pursed her lips together and took a step back. She leaned down and lifted the blade she had been using to spar with. Swiftly, she sliced Eli's left forearm, leaving a gash near his wrist.

"Hey!" Eli yelped in pain. He grabbed at the wound with his right hand and applied pressure. "What the hell was that?"

"Does it hurt?"

"Of course it does. You cut me!"

"Okay, good. We can use that," Demeter said. "Keep your other hand there and think about the pain."

"Easy enough," Eli grumbled, his eyes stinging as they watered.

"Now, I want you to imagine the pain as something physical instead. It could be dirt, a bug, whatever you want it to be. Then, with your other hand, I want you to just wipe it off."

Eli shut his eyes tight and concentrated. He imagined the pain as a caterpillar. He used to love them as a boy, and the sensation of the cut reminded him of how their feet on his arms would tickle so much that it would turn into pain. As he imagined, he moved his hand downward, as if brushing the bug away from himself. When he opened his eyes and looked down again, both the gash and the pain were gone.

Eli was breathless as Demeter grinned at him. It filled him with the most incredible sensation. Warmth and peace surged through his body.

"Okay, so you've mastered healing yourself, at least. I'm a bit indestructible, so we'll have to test healing others a little later. In the meantime, let's move on."

Eli walked with Demeter farther down the track, leaving their weapons behind. As they walked, he gathered his courage to ask her something that had been nagging at him since they met.

"Can I ask you something?"
"Of course, dear," she replied. "That's what I am here for."
"Who was Ales?"

Demeter was quiet for so long that Eli became scared that he overstepped.

"I'm so sorry. It's really none of my business," he blurted.

"It's okay, Eli," she finally spoke, her voice soft. "After reading the prophecy, it's natural that you would be curious. Ales was a mortal man that I loved a long, long time ago. He heard whispers of the prophecy before my siblings, or I did and made it his mission to find the muses. We fought the night before he left.
"The rumors had been that Zeus knew about the prophecy and wanted to keep it hidden. I denied it, vehemently. The brother that I knew could never do something like that. I was wrong, and Ales paid the price. By the time I knew the truth, he was already dead. Zeus found him leaving the muses and sentenced him to be killed so that

no one could ever find what he had learned. I have regretted it ever since."

"I'm so sorry for your loss."

Eli hoped his words conveyed how awful he felt for the goddess. The grief he had felt from his parent's passing was not something he would wish on anyone. And for Demeter to have gone through that, at the hands of family, no less, made Eli want to cry for her.

"Thank you." Demeter stopped walking and turned to him. "Your compassion is a strength. Do not lose sight of it ever."

Eli nodded at her, a silent promise. Just then, a puff of smoke drifted towards them. It swirled around them and then shot into Demeter's ear as if being sucked in somehow. Demeter gave a small smile and then turned to Eli.

"Your friends should be here shortly. Are you ready for your next test?"
"Wait— I mean, yes, I am. What was that, though?" Eli couldn't help his curiosity.
"It's called a Whisper. It's how my siblings and I communicate with each other." She explained. "When we have a message, we simply whisper the name and what we would like them to know. Then it flies to them and, well, you've seen the rest."
"That is so cool." Eli's eyes grew wide. "It's like a mystical Walkie Talkie."
Demeter tilted her head and smiled, bemusedly, "I am not familiar, but I will take your word for it. Now, shall we?"

Suddenly, Demeter transformed. Standing in front of him was no longer a wise goddess in floor-length white robes. It was a little girl with brown pigtails in a pink dress, clutching a teddy bear.

"Your turn," the girl sang. "Close your eyes and focus on anyone or anything."

"Well, I don't want to be a little girl," Eli thought aloud. "But I can try something."

He squeezed his eyes shut once more. Eli wasn't even sure what he was going to think of when he heard Demeter gasp. He opened his eyes, and the goddess was back in her true form, gawking at him. Well, gawking down at him, he should say.

"Wha—" Eli tried to speak but stopped short when he heard a squawk escape his lips instead. He looked down to find his hands were now wings, covered in feathers. He looked up to see Demeter burst into laughter. Filled with panic, Eli ran.

• •

"He turned himself into a chicken?" Lucy had arrived at the track with Theo a few hours later and heard the news. Her eyes were as wide as her grin, and Eli could tell that even Demeter was having trouble stifling her laughter.

"Ahem, hm," the goddess composed herself, "He did very well for his first, ahem, day."

Eli groaned.

"At least you can shapeshift, though." Theo tried to comfort him.

"It's okay, Theo, you guys can laugh."

"Oh, thank heavens," Lucy replied, and the three of them collectively lost their minds to hysterics.

"You— should've seen—" Demeter strained to speak in between giggles and gasps, "He— just started squawking! He ran— so fast. It took me— ages— to catch him!"

"Oh man," Lucy roared, "I would've paid money to see that."

"What on Earth made you turn into a chicken, of all things?" Theo wiped tears from his eyes.

"Oh, uh, I think I was thinking about bacon and eggs."

A lie, indeed, but there was no way Eli was going to tell them that he was thinking about Lucy, and how she had called him an 'egghead' when she had come to kidnap him. He was becoming all too aware of just how many of his thoughts were about Lucy, involuntary or not, but he definitely didn't need anyone else to know that.

There was a moment of silence before Theo spoke up again, asking the question that Eli knew he should've seen coming.

"Does that mean there was a 50/50 chance you would've turned into a pig?"

Laughter erupted once more, this time even Eli joined in with them, chuckling at the absurdity.

"Well," Demeter inhaled, "either way, it was a lightning-fast transition. Very impressive for your first time. Maybe next time, don't think so much about your stomach, and you'll be a pro in no time."

"I'll work on it," Eli smiled at her.

"The others should be here soon," Theo noted, "We can grab food after training since you're apparently starving."

"Before you do that, though," Demeter interrupted, grabbing her sword and making her way to where Lucy stood. "We do still have to test one more thing."

She held up the sword and sliced Lucy across her cheek. Lucy grabbed at her face with both hands, shooting Demeter a look of shock.

"You've gotta be kidding me," Lucy groaned, her face flushing with anger.

"Go on," Demeter gestured to Eli, who then walked over as well. He reached for Lucy's face, and she flinched away from him.

"Trust me?"

Eli removed her hands and replaced them with his own. He thought about the pain she must feel, a bright red caterpillar tiptoeing across her cheek, and he gently wiped it away. With his thumb he traced the skin where the cut had been, avoiding Lucy's gaze, and the electricity he was feeling from standing this close to her.

"See," he remarked quickly, taking a step back, "good as new."

"Yeah, thanks," Lucy touched the spot Eli had just healed, and shook her head, "Maybe next time, you could use Theo for target practice instead."

"Maybe." Demeter agreed, watching Eli with a knowing look on her face.

"Great timing," Eli looked over to where Theo was pointing and saw Wyatt and Liv walking towards them. Their hands intertwined and Liv held onto Wyatt's arm. Eli noted it was the first time he had seen Wyatt smile.

Before they got too close, Eli addressed the others pleadingly, "Can we keep the chicken thing between us, please?"

"Oh, of course, we can," Lucy agreed.

Eli sighed in relief, not noticing the knowing look of defeat on Theo's face.

"Hey, guys," Lucy greeted them. "You'll never guess what Eli did."

■■

In all of Eli's fantasies about going on a magical quest, being a hero, and saving the world, he never once imagined that his journey would lead him to a Denny's in Arkansas. Yet, here he sat, in a booth in the corner, menu in hand. Eli stared out the window, lost in thought, and enjoying the feeling of the sunshine on his face. The Underworld was magnificent, but always nighttime, which made it seem quite cold. Eli loved the sun. He wondered if he got that from Demeter too since she is the Goddess of the harvest. He wished she had come along with them so that he could have talked to her more. He still had so many questions. But she said she had far too much to do, and with the looming threat, he understood.

The whole situation felt surreal to Eli as he sat and recapped the events of the past two days. He was taken to the Underworld, told that he would have to defeat a god, found out he had magical powers, trained with an actual goddess, and now...he was sitting in a diner. At least this was the best location in the state, according to Wyatt, who grew up nearby. While Eli absent-mindedly stirred his coffee, the others were discussing what they might order, which sparked a waffle vs pancake debate amongst the four of them. Eli looked over at Lucy, who was passionately explaining why waffles were better, and why Wyatt was an idiot for disagreeing. As her eyes narrowed and her face grew red, Eli couldn't help but stare.

Of course, Lucy was attractive. He would need to be blind to disagree with the fact. And, if he were being completely honest with himself, he did feel flips in his stomach anytime he saw her smile. But what he had said to Theo was true. With the fate of the world in his hands, this wasn't the time for him to be distracted.

Not a moment too soon, their server appeared, disrupting Eli's thoughts, and pulling him back to the present.

"What can I get ya?" The server flipped open her notebook, pen poised at the ready.

"I will have the waffles," Lucy looked pointedly at Wyatt.

The server clicked her pen, "I'm sorry darlin', we just ran out. Can I get you some pancakes instead?"

"I swear to—" Before she could finish her thought, Theo elbowed Lucy in the side, and instead she muttered, "No, thank you, I will do the scrambled eggs instead. Extra cheese please."

The three boys looked down at their menus, restraining themselves from bursting into laughter, while Liv ordered next. Lucy's face showed indignation as she fiddled with the empty sugar packet in front of her. Wyatt stared at his menu smugly.

Eli was warming up to him. It did seem his awful mood last night was because of Liv. Today, Wyatt was much nicer, not just to Eli, but to everyone else as well. After a few moments, the server finished taking everyone else's orders and left.

"So, besides the poultry issue, how did the rest of your training go?" Liv addressed Eli.

"I think it went okay." He shrugged. "Demeter gave me a golden sword to use on our journey, and I have healing powers, too."

"That's gonna be so useful." Liv gushed. "Isn't that going to be so useful, Wy?"

"Oh yeah," Wyatt smirked, "Super handy."

"What powers do you all have?" Eli asked, "For some reason I assumed they would all be the same."

"You've already seen mine, remember?" Lucy remarked.

"Okay, so, you've got super strength." Eli prodded.

"That's it?" she spat out, insulted. "Who do you think got us here? Or got you to the Underworld in the first place?"

"Lucy can create portals, or doors, to travel between worlds," Theo explained, "Since Hermes is the Messenger God and all."

"Oh, I'm sorry." Eli apologized, "That's impressive, though. What about everyone else?"

At that, the others took turns telling Eli their strengths. Theo got shapeshifting also, and he could duplicate and manipulate any object. It sounded like telekinesis to Eli, and he couldn't hide how impressed he was. Liv explained she could control the sea and, by association, large bodies of water.

"I thought that was Poseidon's thing?" Eli interrupted.

"It is, but it's not only his, just like shapeshifting isn't only Demeter's." Liv clarified. "Aphrodite was born of the sea, so the manipulation of it is her right. She also gave me this super cute belt to wear but told me to only wear it when I absolutely have to."

"A belt?" Eli ventured, glancing at Theo.

"Yeah, specifically a Love Belt," Theo confirmed. "It had belonged to Aphrodite and has the power to cause others to fall in love with the wearer."

Eli wondered if Liv was the best person to own it, but hey, who was he to question Aphrodite's judgment?

"Not to be dismissive," Eli trod carefully, "because those powers sound really great, but how will that help us if we're not near water or trying to sleep with someone?"

Liv laughed, "Yeah, Aphrodite thought about that too. She had been defenseless on a battlefield too many times before. She asked Apollo to give me a sword. He also showed me some basics so that I'm not completely useless."

"Got it," Eli felt relief. "How about you, Wyatt?"

Wyatt took a sip of his coffee before responding, "I can create and manipulate fire, and I have much knowledge. I also got the bow and arrow that Apollo used in the Trojan War, which is pretty cool."

"No way." Eli's eyes widened. "That's the bow with true aim, right?"

"Sure is," Wyatt smirked. "Not that I would've needed it."

It took everything inside of Eli not to roll his eyes at Wyatt's cockiness.

"Wait, what do you mean you have knowledge? How is that a power?"

"It's kinda like a photographic memory, but faster. Like, the average person can read an entire book in about six hours, but I do it in ten seconds and I remember every piece of information I've ever seen. It may not seem like much, but Apollo took me to the hall of records in the Underworld, and now I know every single bit of Greek lore that there's ever been."

"Basically," Lucy followed up, "He's a nerd."

Eli and Theo snickered while Wyatt rolled his eyes at her.

"That's fine, Lucy, but don't come crying to me when you're getting attacked by an Ophiotaurus and you don't know that you're supposed to avoid its entrails."

"Oh, I won't."

"Correct." Wyatt responded, "Because you'll be dead. Because their entrails will have burned you to ash."

Lucy frowned for a moment, then smirked. "Yeah, but then it won't be my problem anymore."

Chapter Seven

"I ate way too much," Eli complained, laying on the living room couch.

Lucy sat across from him in the armchair, hugging her knees to her chest. The others had already gone to their rooms for the night, but Eli was wide awake, even after the long day that he'd had.

"Literally, everyone told you not to get the banana split," Lucy laughed. "I refuse to feel sorry for you."

"Heartless," he joked.

"Cry-baby," she shot back.

Eli stretched out along the length of the couch. "Hey, so, when we met, you told me that Greek myths are real. Does that mean they're all true?"

"What do you mean?" Lucy readjusted, crossing her legs in front of her.

"So, from what I know, Hera and Zeus are always the husband and wife. But aren't they also siblings?" Eli pondered, "And, also, there's a lot of, um, *forced love*, if you know what I mean."

"You mean sexual assault?" Lucy pursed her lips. "Unfortunately, most of it is true. The only difference is no one ever wrote the lore about what came afterward."

"Meaning?"

"They're called Greek Tragedies for a reason. Most mortals back in the old days went through terrible traumas at the hands of the gods. But as the times changed, as more knowledge was available, the gods began reevaluating their outdated logic. Most of them apologized to the women they had assaulted and tried their best to fix it. Apollo is a key example of that. When I first met him, I hated him, and honestly, I might always feel that way. But the fact that he still tries every single day to do better, even at his age, is something I can respect."

"I guess." Eli tried to sort through his conflicting feelings. He had been hoping that there was a better explanation. He didn't understand how Lucy could know, with absolute certainty, that someone had been a monster in that way and somehow find respect for them. It felt like it was just being excused away. After a moment, he decided to just be transparent. "I just feel like there is no way to make up for something like that. An apology doesn't erase the memory or the pain."

"I agree." Lucy tightened her lips into a thin line. "Demeter helped with that part, though, actually. She felt so much guilt for the actions of her brothers that she helped Apollo heal the women's minds and hearts. The two of them talked to each of the women for days, weeks even, and helped them work through it."

Eli couldn't help but feel a twinge of pride.

"As far as the gods sleeping with each other," Lucy segued. "Hermes told me the gods are only parents and siblings in the respect that they all came from the Titans. gods don't share blood or DNA the same way mortals do. But honestly, it's gross and I don't get it, no matter how many times Hermes tried to explain it to me. Luckily, that was something they grew out of too, mostly.

"The only couple still together are Hades and Persephone. While she is technically his niece, the true story is that Demeter had hidden Persephone from the other gods, to protect her, since Zeus was her father and Hera's kind of bitchy. When Hades saw her for the first time, he didn't even fully know that she was a goddess, much less that she was related to him. Zeus knew, but he's a dick, anyway. It wasn't until after she lived with Hades in the Underworld that he found out. But Hera and Zeus aren't together at all now."

"Really? How come?"

"When Zeus proclaimed his plans, the other eleven gods all chose their sides. With him, against him, or staying out of it completely. Hera hated what he was doing and left him. She's not helping us, out of fear, of course. But she's not helping him either, which I appreciate, also out of fear."

"What about the others?" Eli asked.

"I only know about a few of them from Hermes. For sure, Artemis is on our side, but quietly. I've only seen her once since I've been here. Poseidon is holed up in the ocean somewhere. Hephaestus and Ares took Zeus's side, and no one has heard from Athena in over a century. She disappeared right around the time that Ales found the prophecy. I don't think that's a coincidence, though."

Eli exhaled and rubbed his temples, trying to absorb all the information. He decided his other questions would simply have to wait for another time, as his brain was currently overflowing. Lucy watched him, silently.

"Are you not tired?" he asked.

"Nah," Lucy replied, "I'm a night owl, anyway. I probably won't sleep for a few more hours."

"Really? What do you do all night?"

"Wouldn't you like to know?" She winked at him.

"No, you know what I mean," Eli chuckled. "I haven't seen TVs or books around the penthouse. I'm genuinely curious. Do you just stay up all night making mystical doorways?"

Lucy smirked. "If I did, where would you want it to go?"

"I don't even know. I've been to a lot of places."

"Maybe try thinking of somewhere you haven't been."

Eli searched his mind for somewhere interesting. "I mean, I've never been to Amsterdam. That place always seemed cool."

Lucy stood up and stretched her arms above her head, bending her back and then standing up straight.

"Well, come on then."

Eli sat up, curious. "We're not really going to Germany, are we?"

"Why not?" Lucy asked, "I'm not tired, you're not tired. Let's see what trouble we can get into."

She walked over to her bedroom door and waited as Eli slowly rose and made his way to her. She pressed her hand against the wood and, once again, Eli saw the sun-like rays through the cracks. Lucy turned the knob, and the pair stepped over the threshold.

"Welcome to the Van Gogh Museum, Waldo." Lucy giggled. "Where to first?"

They stood in a large room with wooden floors and various pieces of art on the walls. The lights were dimmed around them. Red velvet ropes blocked off portions of the room, and the air smelled of fresh pine cleaner and bleach. They were the only two in the room, the sun setting through the glass windows to their right.

"This is amazing." Eli took a step towards the paintings on the wall.

"I know, right?" Lucy giggled. "And they just closed, so we're gonna have the whole place to ourselves."

"Wait, what?"

A click sounded and the entire room darkened, save for the small lights over the paintings themselves. Eli could hear a whirring sound from above him as Lucy grabbed his arm and pushed them both back up against the wall. He shot her a curious look, and she nodded to the paintings. As Eli looked across to them, he could see tiny ripples of red and realized they were infrared alarms. He had only ever seen them before in movies.

"Can't you do your door thing and get us back to the penthouse?" Eli asked.

"I could, but…" Lucy stopped for a second.

"But, what?"

"I just feel like that's no fun, honestly."

With that, Lucy took a step forward and the entire building lit up once more, this time with alarms blaring. She turned to Eli and held out her hand, a grin on her face.

"You coming?"

Eli grabbed her hand, and they ran.

■■

Eli and Lucy took the exit to the stairs and ran down three flights before finally finding an unlocked storage closet to take refuge in. The space was so small they were practically nose to nose.

"You're crazy." Eli panted. "They're gonna find us any minute."

"Let them," Lucy giggled, "We'll just portal out. You've got to admit, it's a rush."

"Most illegal things are, I hear."

"Eli, we've got gods-given powers. There are no consequences here. Watch."

Lucy placed her hand up to the door, but this time, no light came through. She tried the knob to find the door had locked when they closed it behind them.

"What's happening?" Eli's voice wavered.

"So, funny story," Lucy nervously chuckled. "My powers are a little limited."

"What do you mean, limited?"

"Well, we're not actual gods, are we?" she scoffed. "I can't make portals the way Hermes can. And, well, I can't make them if the door gets locked."

"Are you joking?" Eli exclaimed, fear gripping him. "What were you going to do when they threw us in a locked jail cell?"

"I honestly didn't think we would get caught."

"Well, this is just great." Eli leaned against the wall and slid down it, sitting on the ground. Lucy stepped around him and sat as well.

The two sat in silence for what felt like forever to Eli. When he finally looked over at Lucy, he saw her eyes filled with unease. In the brief time he had known her, he had only ever seen her strong. Laughing, teasing, sarcastic, and angry. The sight created a lump in his throat.

"Hey, we really will be okay." He nudged her shoulder with his. "We're prophesied to save the world, not die in a German prison."

"Yeah, I know." She replied, sighing. "I was just thinking of something else."

"Oh, yeah?"

"It's nothing."

"We're kinda stuck in here for a bit. Might as well make conversation," Eli prodded.

Lucy lifted her head and stared straight ahead.

"I've been here before," she began. "Not here physically, but in this situation. It just didn't work out so well the last time."

"What happened?"

"I'm sure you already know by now that I grew up in the foster system."

"Oh, I—"

"It's okay, if Theo told you, I mean. It wasn't a secret." She assured him, sighing. "I grew up in Henderson, Nevada. No family ever took me or anything, so I aged out at 18. I started hanging with the wrong crowd and found out I have a knack for sleight of hand. Another gods-given gift, I guess. I tried to get an actual job, but nothing ever worked out, so I had to make money by taking some odd jobs that required more of a criminal skill set."

Eli's eyes widened, surprised.

"At first it was just counting cards at a few small casinos in Vegas." Lucy continued. "But one of my friends, Jeremy, wanted to do something bigger. He was way stronger than me, at the time, and a lot scarier. I wanted to say no, but I was sure if I did that, he'd kill me. Long story short, we ended up trapped together in a bank vault."

"Jeez," Eli whispered. "How did you get out?"

"I got lucky, I guess. Jeremy did not. He tried to run as soon as the doors opened, and they shot him. Two bullets and he was gone. The DA took pity on me since I was so young, and it was technically my first offense. I got a few months in jail and three years of community service."

"That's insane." Eli thought aloud. "I'm so sorry."

"It is what it is."

Instinctively, he reached over and grabbed her hand, holding it in his. He thought about the caterpillar. He wasn't sure at all that this would work on a pain that wasn't physical. At that moment, all Eli knew was that he wanted nothing more than to take her worries and sadness away.

"Thank you," Lucy sighed, and laid her head back down on his shoulder.

"Anytime."

Just then, the handle on the door began jiggling, and they could hear a man yelling in German from the outside. The two jumped up and apart, Lucy looking over at Eli.

"I'm going first. You'll know when to run."

Eli nodded in understanding. As soon as the door opened, Lucy rushed forward and used all of her strength to knock the security guard backward. He fell to the ground, lying there unconscious.

Eli moved to Lucy, grabbed her hand, and together they ran.

■■■

The pair made it to the end of a long hallway and turned the corner, skidding to a halt as three more security guards blocked their way. They turned back, sprinting in the other direction. Eli glimpsed something out of the corner of his eye and couldn't help but stop.

"Eli," Lucy hissed at him. She stomped back to where he stood.

"Sunflowers." Eli grinned at the painting on the wall in front of them. "The real Sunflowers painting."

Lucy huffed, "Great, we can come back during open hours and see it then. We have to go!"

Using her super strength, she grabbed his arm and dragged him a few feet forward, nearly picking him completely off the ground. Once Eli snapped out of it, he began running alongside her once more. As soon as they were far enough ahead, Lucy grabbed his hand and pulled him around a corner, stopping them both.

"Why are we stopping now?" he asked. "Did you see a painting you like, too?"

"No. Luckily, only one of us has the attention span of a fly." She spat. "But I have an idea. You need to shape-shift into the guard I knocked out."

"What about you, though?"

"You'll tell them you caught me, and that you're escorting me to jail." She said simply.

"I don't speak German."

"Once you switch, you probably will. You didn't know how to squawk like a chicken before that happened, either."

"I don't think it works that way."

"Do you have a better idea?"

He did not. Eli squeezed his eyes shut and grew concerned when he heard Lucy's scoff. He opened his eyes, now looking up at her, with wings where his arms should be.

"Man, what is up with you and chickens?"

Eli clucked in frustration.

"Shit, they're coming." Lucy peeked around the corner. She looked down at Eli and glared. "I would like to make it known; I really didn't want to have to do it this way."

Eli watched helplessly as she fought the guards in a flurry of fists and elbows, with a couple of kicks thrown in. With her overpowered strength, it was a quick fight, though. At one point, the larger security guard grabbed her around the neck from behind. Lucy shifted her weight slightly and pulled the guard over her shoulder, sending him flying out in front of her. Once the guards were all unconscious, she came back to Eli, showing no signs that she had just been in a fight at all.

Eli clucked at her, pecking lightly at her feet.

"Oh, it's okay, little noodle. You can change back now. Just focus hard on being yourself."

Eli closed his eyes and was relieved when he looked down and he was back in his true form.

"Noodle?" Eli inquired.
"Yeah, like, Chicken Noodle."

They looked at each other for a moment, and then they both laughed.

"Okay, we have to find an unlocked door."

"I think I see a stairwell down that way." Eli pointed to the end of the hallway, and they sprinted towards it.

Lucy tried the handle once they got there and luckily it turned. She placed her hand on it, and moments later, the pair were back in the Perished Pub.

Lucy slammed the door behind them, and the pair took a beat, trying to slow their breathing. Eli had never felt more exhilarated in his life and looking over at Lucy only made his breathlessness worse.

Eli watched as Lucy flounced over to the bartender to call for a car. He ignored the onlookers who were staring at him strangely, knowing what a mess he must look like at the moment.

The door behind him opened and a brunette woman stepped through, stopping as she noticed Eli.

"Oh, hey, Eli. You know everyone's looking for you, right?"

"I'm sorry? Who are you?"

"Artemis!" Lucy's voice called from the bar. She nodded to the bartender and walked back over, embracing the woman once she approached. "What on earth are you doing here?"

"I was just telling Eli; everyone's been looking for you guys. Something's happened, I've got to get you two back to the penthouse."

"Wait, you're Artemis?" Eli shook his head, trying to catch up.

"The one and only." The goddess grinned. "It's a pleasure to meet you, kid, but we really have to get back."

"The car should be here any second," Lucy said, and the trio began heading towards the front door. "What's going on?"

"I think it's best if Apollo explains. I don't admit this often, but for once he actually knows much more than me."

Chapter Eight

As the elevator doors opened up to the Penthouse, pure chaos greeted the trio stepping out of them. Eli's eyes were being pulled in all directions, trying to make sense of what he was seeing.

Theo and Wyatt were running back and forth from their rooms to the living room, piling several duffel bags onto the couches. Liv was in the kitchen, unpacking bags of food and stocking the refrigerator and pantry. Eli looked at Lucy in confusion. They couldn't eat here, why would she need to do that? Lucy didn't catch his glance, her eyes focused on the shouting coming from the other side of the room.

Dionysus and Demeter stood around the dining table with three others whom Eli did not recognize. They were looking at the center of the table as they argued loudly amongst themselves.

"We have no choice; it has to be now." Demeter asserted, her eyes pleading with the others.

"They're not ready!" A tall blond man argued. "And on top of that they haven't even had any sleep, they're going to be completely useless."

"They are ready." Dionysus interjected. "And even if they weren't, Zeus doesn't care. This is happening, no matter what your fancy timetable says, Apollo."

Artemis walked quickly over to the bickering group, Lucy and Eli trailing behind her.

"You lot were shouting when I left you, too. Do you never run out of steam?"

The group turned as they approached, Demeter's eyes lighting up as she saw Eli. Lucy walked over and hugged the shorter of the three men.

"Oh, thank heavens you found them." Demeter hugged Artemis before turning to Eli. "Elias, I don't believe you've met my nephews and niece just yet. This is Hermes, Apollo, and Aphrodite." She introduced, pointing to each of them, respectively.

Hermes was shorter than Eli had pictured, but he held himself as if he were seven feet tall. Apollo had to have been almost seven feet tall. His face was stoic, and he seemed very no-nonsense. Then came Aphrodite. Tall, regal, elegant. Everything he had ever read about her did not do her justice in the least.

"Hello, it is very nice to meet you all," Eli said politely.
"Demeter, you said he'd bow. He didn't bow." Hermes looked disappointed.
"Oh, jeez, I'm so sorry," Eli leaped to his feet and bowed at the waist, earning him chuckles from the gods and goddesses.
"I'm just joking, boy, it's quite alright."

Eli stood up straight, his face red. He should've realized, he thought, considering Lucy was his descendant. Of course, Hermes was just messing with him.

"What is happening, Hermes?" Lucy addressed her descendant, moving her eyes over the papers in the center of the table.

"We've received word that Zeus is planning to make his move sooner than we had anticipated. He is sending Ares and his army into the Underworld to capture the Five before you have a chance to begin your journey."

"I thought he couldn't reach us here." Lucy shook her head. "Isn't that why we've been living here all this time?"

"He could always come here," Aphrodite spoke up. "He wouldn't though because entering into Hades' territory would be seen as an act of war."

"And it's not now?" Eli inquired.

"Oh, it still is," the goddess continued, "but Zeus is so close to exacting his plan that he no longer cares."

Eli shuddered, his heart beating faster.

"What are these?" He asked, pointing to the mess of papers on the dining room table. Some pages were completely filled up while others had fractured paragraphs and sentences scrawled across them.

"Since the prophecy was discovered," Apollo began, "we've had seers assisting us whenever they could. They aren't always able to give us a full reading, which is why some of the pages only have a few sentences. It's always been sort of like a road map torn into puzzle pieces that we have to put together. We've just been going over them to find anything that could possibly help us."

"And?" Lucy asked.

"Nothing." Dionysus sighed. "Not one damn sentence

in here tells us what our next course of action should be, which is why we're divided at the moment."

Eli began to understand why they were arguing but was terrified to hear them say it out loud. He wanted to shout that he needed more time. None of this was fair and he wasn't ready for any of it to be true.

"The Five must leave tonight." Demeter determined, confirming Eli's fears. "It's the only way. If Ares gets here first, all of this was for nothing."

"Demeter," Apollo warned. "We need to discuss this. I understand you have seniority but—"

"I do have seniority." Her green eyes flashed. "Zeus is my brother, my responsibility. I care about these children just as much as the rest of you, but your fears are what's going to get them killed right now. You know that I'm right about this."

Apollo stood in silence for a moment before dropping Demeter's gaze and turning back to the table.

"Fine. Lucia, Elias, go now, please."

"Lucia?" Eli couldn't help but smirk as the pair walked away from the table.

"Elias?" Lucy countered.

"Fair enough." He laughed. "Hey, why is Liv stocking the kitchen, do you know?"

"Food for the journey," she began to explain as they reached the door to Eli's room. "Hermes created a portal between our kitchen and my bag so if we ever need food or something to drink, I can just grab it wherever we are."

"Okay, and what about our beds? Or do we get a portal for those too?"

"No, dummy. We have money for a hotel, and if there's not one around, we have tents and sleeping bags."

Eli swallowed hard. There were many unknowns still lingering around them, so much so that thousands of questions were bumping into each other in his head, trying to find a way out. Lucy must have sensed his concern because she reached out and placed a hand on his arm.

"I know that worrying is kind of your thing," she said gently, "but I promise, we've had these plans in place for months. There are a lot of things we don't know, but we've thought of everything that we can."

Eli nodded. Lucy gave him one last smirk before leaving him to pack. Eli went through the dresser drawers and took all the clothes he could find, not even sure what he needed to bring, and picked up his golden sword that was still in the sheath Demeter had given him and fastened it to his side. He double-checked he wasn't forgetting anything, grabbed his bag, and went out into the living room. Theo and Wyatt were already sitting on the couch, their bags on the floor in front of them.

"We may need to stop for coffee on the way." Eli sat his bag on the ground and collapsed in the armchair.
"If we have time," Theo assured.
"Or, you could've gotten some sleep like the rest of us instead of going on a late-night portal adventure with Red." Wyatt rolled his eyes.
"Oh, yeah, because I could've guessed any of this would happen." Eli retorted sarcastically. "Not all of us have the grand gift of knowledge, douchebag."
Wyatt laughed. "Yeah, obviously."

"Children." Apollo approached the trio before Eli could respond to Wyatt's insult. The boys stood as the god reached them. "Are we almost ready?"
"Just waiting on the girls," Wyatt responded.

As Wyatt spoke, Liv and Lucy entered the living room, bags slung over their shoulders.

"No worries, we're ready," Liv announced.

Apollo turned to his family with a look of worry on his face.

"As soon as we leave, you each need to go as well. Keep in contact. If *anything* goes wrong at all send a Whisper. I should meet up with you all tomorrow afternoon."

"Wait," Eli turned to Demeter, "Are you not coming with us?"

"Unfortunately, we cannot," Demeter replied sadly. "The more people who go the larger the chance of being found is. Apollo will join you to help you all get started, and I assure you, Eli, you're in very good hands."

Eli felt his face fall in disappointment. Demeter stepped closer to him and wrapped him in a hug. He inhaled the scent of wildflowers and did his best to not tear up, knowing that it was stupid. After losing his parents and being on his own for years, being with Demeter was a gift. Her kindness and support opened something up in Eli, and he wasn't ready to let go of that just yet.

"Everything will be okay," she assured, before letting go. "Stay together. Stay safe."

"We will," Eli promised, clearing his throat.

He stood by as he watched the others say their goodbyes to their ancestors as well. Dionysus and Theo shared a quick hug, slapping each other's backs like you might see college boys do at a frat party. Lucy did not embrace Hermes, opting instead to joke about how awful he was going to miss her. Aphrodite and Liv shared a long hug.

"Well?" Lucy placed a pair of sunglasses on her head and asked, "Are we leaving to save the world, or what?"

Chapter Nine

Eli took in a deep breath and stared in awe at his surroundings. The lush green grass met the mountains to his right. To his left he could see the ocean, the sun sparkling off of the deep blue waves, the white foam crashing on the shore. The air smelled of fresh-cut grass and sea salt, a delicious combination that Eli had never encountered before.

Apollo and The Five had taken one of Lucy's portals to the Plain of Thessaly after leaving the penthouse the night before. The doorway led to a nearby monastery where they were able to get a few hours of sleep before Apollo woke them to leave.

"Are you okay?" Eli asked Apollo as the group walked out to the center of the plains. He noticed the god seemed on edge, fiddling with his bag and glancing left to right quickly.

"I am fine," Apollo stated firmly. "I am simply being cautious. If I am caught right now, they will cart me off to Tartarus, which would mean I would have to cancel my golf game with Hestia. She will assume it's because I don't want to lose again and rub it in my face for eternity."

The god spoke jokingly, but Eli could sense a hint of genuine worry behind his words. The last thing he wanted was for any of their ancestors to get in trouble.

Apollo cleared his throat and addressed the entire group. "This is the battle site where the Olympians fought and defeated the Titans in a ten-year war. It only makes sense that this is where your journey should begin as well."

"What was the war about?" Liv asked.

"To see which group would be the rulers of the Universe." Wyatt chimed in, earning a look of pride from Apollo.

"Also," Apollo added, "my grandfather was the worst."

Once they reached the center, Apollo guided the Five into a row, sorting Theo, Lucy, Eli, Liv, and Wyatt in that order.

"Now, you must all join hands, and the path will appear." Apollo took a step back behind them, giving Wyatt a slight nod as he did.

Eli grabbed Lucy and Wyatt's hands and waited. After a moment, nothing had happened, and when Eli heard Lucy scoff, he looked over and saw why. Theo would not grab Lucy's hand.

"You okay?" Eli leaned over to ask.

Theo stood frozen in place, his breathing heavy and rapid. Eli stepped forward and guided Lucy to switch places with him. He placed his hand on Theo's shoulder, as Theo had done for him many times before.

"I don't think I can do this." Theo's voice quivered. "Talking about it was one thing, that's all it was. But we have to actually go do it now and…"

"We've got you," Eli promised him. "We're all in this together, right?"

Theo swallowed hard and finally looked up. He nodded at Eli and muttered an apology to the others.

As soon as Eli and Theo's hands joined, an enormous amount of energy rippled through his body. As he held on to the other's hands, he could tell it was affecting them, too. Then, right before their eyes, a large golden archway materialized. The sides looked like columns, heavily encircled by vines and roses. There was a pathway, also golden, leading out of it, and towards the East.

"Well, I guess that's our direction," Wyatt said, and the Five dropped their hands.

"Where is it pointing you to?" Apollo asked them.

"Can you not see it?" Lucy asked the god

"I cannot," he replied. "Only the Five can. That will help you on your journey as well, so as not to attract the attention of anyone else."

"Well, it's going that way."

Apollo looked at where Lucy was pointing and nodded.

"It's taking you towards Elitsa, which will be about a three-day journey. Once you arrive there, you will need to find passage on a ship going in the same direction as the path. That will be the tricky part since the Isle of Extinction is difficult to find, and not on any map. With the direction you gave me, you'll want to find a ship sailing towards Megalonisi."

Apollo reached into his bag and pulled out a map and five ID cards. He handed the map to Wyatt and the ID cards to Theo.

"Hermes had one fake ID made for each of you, with your new aliases." Apollo continued. "Be careful who you trust on your journey. By now, anyone important will have heard of the prophecy, which means Zeus could place dangers in your way if one of his acolytes finds you."

"Dangers?" Eli asked.

"Have you read The Odyssey, Elias?" Apollo asked.

"Understood."

The god reached into his bag once more and pulled out a small coin pouch. It jangled as he wordlessly handed it off to Wyatt, giving the boy a meaningful look. Wyatt took the pouch and simply nodded in response, putting it in his bag.

Apollo's ears perked up and, moments later, several voices loudly shouting came from over a hill nearby. The skies above them darkened, and Apollo addressed them all once more.

"Now, you must be on your way. I fear I've been with you for too long already. Watch out for each other and stay true to your mission." Apollo then turned back to Wyatt. "It has been an honor."

"What's going on?" Wyatt asked, concerned.

Eli stared at the hill as a large group of men with shields and swords marched over top of it and towards them.

"Those are hoplites." Wyatt panicked. "Greek soldiers that work with Ares."

"You must all go now," Apollo commanded.

"What about you?" Theo argued.

"I appreciate your concern, but I can handle myself."

Apollo smiled. "I'll hold them off, but you all need to go."

"Won't they throw you in Tartarus?" Lucy asked.

"If they wanted to do that, they should've sent Ares himself. I can take them on, no problem." Apollo turned to Wyatt. "I'll see you soon, I promise."

Wyatt hastily gave Apollo one last hug. "Give 'em hell."

Apollo nodded. "You as well."

The Five all nodded to the god before turning to run down the golden path. Once they were almost out of the clearing and into the woods, Eli turned back to make sure they weren't being chased, but the hoplites solely focused on Apollo.

Apollo's grin as he fought the soldiers was the last thing Eli saw before he turned back to face forward, running with his friends towards their mission.

Chapter Ten

It had been only an hour since the group had left Thessaly, and Eli hated to admit it, but he agreed with Liv. After the path led them from the plains, the woods opened up next to a country road. They had been sticking to the side of the road ever since, and the rocks were jabbing into Eli's shoes like tire spikes. He had an idea that he was out of shape, but the burning in his chest is what drove it home for him.

"I'm not trying to complain," Liv huffed, "but I'm already dying."

"Don't be so dramatic." Theo chuckled, "We just started."

Wyatt stopped the group and handed Liv a water bottle. "I think there's a town about a mile up. We can look for a car there."

There was a collective sigh of relief, followed by laughter as they realized they all felt the same. They set off again and, sure enough, the town came into view as they walked farther ahead.

Eli and Theo split off from the group to grab snacks from a nearby grocer, while Wyatt, Lucy, and Liv headed to the car rental company since Wyatt was the only one of them who could speak Greek. The inside of the grocery store was freezing, and the different snacks and cuisines lining the aisles overwhelmed Eli. He looked over and saw Theo already carrying several items.

"Can you read any of this?" He asked Theo. "I have no clue what I'm even looking at."
"Nah, but I think it's all edible, so I'm just grabbing what I can." Theo chuckled.

Eli nodded and followed suit, grabbing what looked like small snack cakes and a few sandwiches. He stopped at the drinks and pulled out a few small bottles. He wasn't sure if it was juice or soda, but the colors looked enticing.

Once the boys paid for the groceries, they headed over to find the others. Luckily, the buildings were right next to one another, so they didn't have to carry their food very far. They stepped inside the rental office to find Wyatt signing paperwork. Lucy and Liv noticed them enter and stepped over to them to help carry their bags.

"How's it going here?" Theo asked.
"It's all Greek to me," Liv jested. "But Wyatt's been doing paperwork for a few minutes now, so hopefully it's going well."

Just then Wyatt finished and handed the papers over to the man behind the counter, who presented him with a set of keys. Wyatt nodded to the man and then turned to the others.

"Alright, before anyone says a word, I'm driving. Let's go."
"Ooh, shotgun!" Liv exclaimed.

The Five walked out into the parking lot to find a silver car waiting for them. They threw their bags in the trunk and piled inside the car. As Wyatt pulled out of the lot, Eli noticed something felt wrong deep in his stomach.

"Uh, guys?"

"Yeah. I feel it too," Lucy answered. "I don't think we should do this."

"Oh, come on. I get it coming from Worrywart Waldo, but you too, Lucy?" Theo sighed. "This is the easiest and fastest way to get there. Walking will take days."

Eli pursed his lips and he and Lucy both sat back. He agreed with Theo and didn't want to walk the whole way either, but the feeling in his gut would not subside.

"Fine." Eli relented. "Maybe we just have motion sickness or something."

"No," Wyatt stopped the car. "You're both right. Look, the path is gone."

As Eli looked up at the front of the car, he noticed where Wyatt was pointing. The path had completely disappeared. As soon as the car was parked, he stepped out of it and the path returned. He sat back down inside the vehicle, and it vanished once more.

"The path will forge beneath our feet." Wyatt recited. "I guess it's literal."

"Stupid prophecy," Liv mumbled as she exited the vehicle, slamming the door behind her.

■ ■

It had been several hours since the Five left the rental car company on foot, and Eli was feeling it now. With every step on the side of the interstate, he imagined he was walking over sharp, jagged rocks, and his stomach was growling, yearning to be fed.

He lagged back from the rest of the group, taking slower steps so as not to fall over. Lucy must've noticed because she hung back as well. He glanced up and saw the evening glow of sunlight shining in her hair. It took most of the strength he had left to not stare, focusing on their shoes instead. As they walked in silence, Eli steadied himself and fell into a rhythm with her footsteps.

"You look as tired as I feel," she noted.
"Maybe a late-night adventure to Amsterdam, before going on the most important adventure of our lives, wasn't the best idea." Eli teased.
"Do you regret it?" She asked.

Eli thought about the intimate moment they had shared in the storage closet. His stomach felt queasy. Butterflies, he realized.

"I don't," he replied honestly, "but my feet might."

He realized he was not the only one feeling this way as Wyatt pulled out the map.

"We need to find somewhere to stop for the night," Wyatt said, studying the atlas.
"That's the best news I've heard all week," Liv enthused, "I may start crying."

Lucy and Theo chimed in their agreement as well.

"Is there somewhere close by that looks safe?" Eli inquired.

Wyatt nodded. "It's slightly out of the way, but Tachydromeon Square is a few blocks up. They'll have food and hotels."

"Sounds good to me," Eli said. "Lead the way."

The other four followed Wyatt and his map a few more blocks before finally arriving at the square. They looked around and chose to stay the night at the Grand Hotel, mainly because it was the cheapest.

"As always, I'll do the talking when we get in there," Wyatt said.

"Show-off," Lucy mumbled.

"Learn Greek." Wyatt shot back.

Once inside the lobby, the group walked up to the receptionist's desk.

"How many rooms?" The hotel desk clerk looked up from her computer, peering up over her horn-rimmed glasses. She spoke perfect English, which made Lucy turn her head and snicker. Wyatt rolled his eyes in response.

"Four, please."

The woman clicked a few times with her mouse and turned around to the printer. She grabbed the freshly printed pages and then four keys hanging on the hooks above, laying them out in front of Wyatt.

"ID and form of payment, please."

Wyatt handed her his fake ID and a gold card. After studying the ID, she made a copy and swiped the gold card.

"Down the hall and to your left." She stated, handing both cards back.

Wyatt picked up the papers and keys and distributed them. The group walked down the hall and found their rooms, stopping outside their respective doors.

"It's nearly seven now, so plenty of time to get some sleep. Let's plan to meet in my room in the morning. 7:30?" Theo suggested. Eli immediately felt a sense of dread.
"Is the sun even up then?" He groaned.
"I'll grab a bag of coffee from the portal." Lucy nudged Eli's shoulder. "See you all tomorrow."

She disappeared into her room, and Wyatt and Liv followed suit. Theo looked at where Lucy had stood previously and then back at Eli suspiciously.

"Want a drink, Waldo?"
Eli closed his eyes and nodded. "I really do."
"Hell yeah." Theo pumped his fist in the air. "Bro's night! I'll let Wyatt know."
"Do you have to?" Eli groaned.
"It'll be fun, trust me. Get cleaned up and meet me back here in thirty."

Eli chuckled, shaking his head. He entered his room and threw his duffel onto his bed. Searching through it, he found a nice pair of jeans and a blue button-down shirt.

"Thank you, Netherworld Express."

Eli changed his clothes, running a comb through his hair and throwing on some deodorant as well. He looked himself over in the mirror and, while he wasn't exactly ready for the red carpet, he also didn't look like he had been hiking for nine hours.

"Well, I'll take what I can get." He muttered at his reflection.

Chapter Eleven

Theo led Eli and Wyatt down a cobblestone street that ran parallel to their hotel. A string of white lights hung across the gap in the rooftops above them, dimly lighting their path. Eli couldn't help but look up as he walked, entranced by the way they twinkled against the pitch-black sky. About a block away, the boys stopped in front of a small brick building with a bistro out front, and a neon sign that blinked the name "Nectar".

The windows had a dark tint to them, and a large man with a black shirt and an earpiece stood just outside the entrance. A doorman? Eli wondered to himself skeptically. It seemed strange to have security at the front door of such a small place, but the man stopped them just as they approached the door, confirming Eli's theory.

"Reason?" the man asked gruffly. His face was completely void of expression.

Eli looked at Wyatt and Theo in confusion. Wyatt had a look of uncertainty as well, but Theo grinned and faced the man.

"Do we even need one?"

The man flashed a toothy smile at the boys and stepped to the side, allowing them to enter.

As soon as the man opened the doors, Eli could hear a loud bass thumping out a dance song. The boys entered, and Eli stared at his surroundings in disbelief. As if by magic, the inside of the building was three times the size of the outside. There was a DJ set up at the back of the room, where hundreds of people were dancing while bright lights strobed above.

Along both sides of the room were shelves upon shelves of alcohol, and there were dozens of couches set up where people passed around hookah hoses.

"Where the hell are we?" Eli shouted to Theo over the music.

"Dionysus brought me here a few months back. Isn't it so cool?" Theo bobbed his head along to the music. "Everyone here is a mythical creature or someone who knows one, mostly nymphs. The guy at the front door is there to keep the mortals from finding out. That's why we needed the passphrase to get in."

"Guys, check this out! This is so cool." Wyatt called from the bar. Theo and Eli walked over as well, sitting on the two empty stools beside him. "It just knows what you want, somehow!"

As soon as Eli sat down, a shot glass full of blue liquid appeared in front of him. He looked over at Theo and saw that he had a shot as well, but with green liquid inside.

"Is this safe?" Eli sniffed at the shot, crinkling his nose, as the smell of pure alcohol entered his nostrils.
"I hope so," Wyatt answered. "Mine tasted delicious."

"No, I mean, that too. But being out in the open at a place like this. What if someone recognizes us?"

"Eli, you need to stop worrying so much," Theo smirked before throwing back his shot and slamming the glass down. "Relax and take the shot. I guarantee it's exactly what you need."

Eli held the cup in his hands and sloshed the drink around. Maybe Theo was right, and he needed to relax. Plus, he thought to himself, if this goes wrong, I've only got a few days left. Might as well make the most of it. He downed the shot, surprised that it didn't burn his throat like he was expecting. It didn't even taste like alcohol at all, but rather like a blueberry candy.

"You know, Waldo," Wyatt slurred. "You're actually an okay guy."

"Then why are you such a dick to me all the time?"

The words shot out of Eli's mouth with no forethought, and he couldn't understand why, but he felt no guilt or fear over what he said.

"At first, I really thought it was because I just didn't like you." Wyatt reached for another shot. "But upon introspection and alcohol, it may be because I've been given shit my whole life for being a know-it-all, so eventually I just started being a jerk before anyone else could be a jerk to me."

"That, one hundred percent, does not make it okay, man." Eli noticed he was slurring a bit as well.

"True." Wyatt's head perked up. "Hey, you guys wanna go dance? I wanna go dance."

By the time Eli opened his mouth to respond, Wyatt was already making his way to the stage.

"Okay, what's actually in these?"

"Whatever you need most," Theo smirked. "It seems like Wyatt needed perspective. Or maybe just to be honest with someone, who knows? What did you need?"

"Probably just the alcohol, honestly." Eli laughed.

Out of the corner of his eye, he noticed a woman watching him from the end of the bar. As she caught his gaze, she smiled flirtatiously and raised her glass to him.

"I think I'm in love with Lucy." Eli blurted out.

When he received no response, he looked over to find Theo was no longer seated beside him. Eli scanned the room but didn't see either of his friends.

"Oh well," he grabbed his next shot, "more for me."

"Save me one." The woman had made her way over and was now seated directly beside him, downing her pink drink.

"I'm sorry?"

"You don't need to be. My name's Callie."

"I'm Eli.'

- -

"So, this Lucy, why haven't you told her how you feel yet?"

Eli and Callie sat on a brown leather couch, passing a hookah hose between them. Eli had never had hookah before, and he coughed the first time he tried, but after a few puffs, he got used to it. He didn't mind the fruity taste and the way the smoke floated into shapes as he exhaled, his fingers gliding through the vapors. He also didn't mind Callie's company, he noticed.

"It's kind of bad timing," Eli answered. "Plus, I doubt she feels the same. She's super flirty but she never actually talks about actual emotions, so it's hard to tell."

"Maybe someone hurt her previously." Callie took a long drag from the hose, exhaling an enormous cloud of smoke from between her bright red lips. The look on her face made Eli believe she was speaking from experience. "A lot of girls have a hard time letting anyone in after that. Do you know if she had another boyfriend recently?"

Eli ignored the pounding in his chest at the thought of Lucy with another guy. "I really don't know that much about her. Like I said, she keeps to herself."
"Maybe that's your first hurdle, then."
"What do you mean?"
"Well if you don't know that much about her, how can you know you're not simply falling in love with the idea of her?" Callie tilted her head. "So far it sounds like you know some of her and you're just guessing at the rest. But she's not a journal for you to fill in, Eli. She has her own story, thoughts, and opinions. Talking to her about that should be your first step."

Is she right? Is that what I've been doing? Eli reached for the hose and paused with it just outside of his lips.

"I hope this isn't rude to ask but, what are you, anyway?"
"What am I?" Callie raised her brows.
"Yeah. If this place is just for myths and friends, which one are you?"

The girl ran her hand through her long brown hair, eyes looking up at the ceiling in thought.

"I'm a friend to you. I think that should matter more than my DNA."

"It does, for sure. I was just curious. I'm sorry if I overstepped." And he was sorry. It had been great talking to her, and now he felt like a complete jackass.

"Have another shot," Callie smirked and pointed down at the table to where another blue drink awaited him. "You're apologizing again."

"Fair enough." Eli laughed and obeyed, throwing his head back as he drank. He set the glass back down and looked back up at her. "You know, you're really pretty."

Callie laughed and placed her hand on his knee. She leaned forward, and before Eli could react, her lips were on his. The kiss was pleasant, but it was nothing compared to the electricity he felt when he was simply standing near Lucy. It was nice, though. It had been a while since someone showed him affection in this way, a while since he had even opened himself up to the possibility. Eli gave in, enjoying the feeling of Callie's embrace. He wrapped his arms around her, pulling her in closer.

She pulled away slightly, and breathed, "Do you wanna get out of here?"

He did, but Lucy's face in his head stopped him in his tracks. At that moment, he knew he only wanted to get back to her. Callie was great, but Eli knew she was just a placeholder for what he truly wanted, and that felt unfair to everyone involved.

After allowing himself a few more seconds of closeness, he pulled away with a sigh and reached for Callie's hand, holding it in his.

"I meant what I said. You are gorgeous. But you're not Lucy."

Callie had a smile on her face as she squeezed Eli's hand.

"You're not who I wanted either, no offense. But it was nice getting to know you, Eli"

She stood from her cushion and smirked.

"Have a great night. Lucy's a very lucky girl."
Eli smiled at her and nodded. "You too, Callie."

Eli blew another puff of smoke and, as the smoke cleared, he saw Theo across the room, watching him with a look of surprise and amusement.

"Well, that's just great."

■■

"I can't believe that out of the three of us, Worrywart Waldo is the one who hooked up tonight." Wyatt remarked, stumbling beside Eli and Theo down the block and back towards their hotel.
"If we could not say that so loudly, that would be great," Eli replied.
"Come on, Eli. Lucy's nowhere near us." Theo chuckled. "We all know that's what you're worried about, whether you can admit it or not."
"I'll admit it if we can all just shut up about it." Eli groaned, reaching out to steady Wyatt. "Jeez, how many shots did he have?"
"Enough." Wyatt giggled.

The boys made their way inside their hotel and down the hallway to their rooms. Eli and Theo both shushed Wyatt the entire way. As soon as Wyatt was safely in his room, Theo and Eli stepped over to their doors.

"Don't worry, Eli. He's not gonna remember by tomorrow, and I won't say a thing." Theo smiled. "But you shouldn't be ashamed. She was hot. What was her name?"

"Callie," Eli responded in a hushed tone, certain that he was too close to where Lucy slept to talk about this.

Theo's eyes grew wide, and he let out a laugh.

"Wait, what? Why are you laughing?" Eli demanded.

"No reason Waldo. It's a nice name, that's all. Have a good night."

Theo unlocked his door, still laughing, and disappeared inside. Eli shook his head, rolled his eyes, and disappeared into his room as well, heading straight for the bathroom and turning on the shower.

Eli stepped into the tub, glad to feel the warm water soothe his aches from the hike and his stomach from the drinks. As he was drying off, there was a knock on his door. He went to it and looked through the peephole. It was blurry, but the reddish-blonde blob was unmistakable.

Oh, shit, she knows.

"Uh, one second." Eli rushed to put on his pajamas. The last thing he needed was for Lucy to see him half-naked right now. After he got dressed, he opened the door.

"Hey there, Lucy." Eli tried to play it cool but ended up leaning against the doorway in an awkward pose. "What brings you by at this time of night?"

"It's only 9…" Eli noticed the gray in her eyes darken

as she looked at him curiously. "Are you okay?"

"Yeah, totally fine. You look great, by the way, I like your hair like that." Eli pointed to Lucy's head, her long hair flowing freely down her back. It was the first time Eli had ever seen it not pulled up into a ponytail.

"Uh, okay, weirdo. Anyway, the AC in my room broke." Lucy gestured to the pillow and blanket in her arms. Eli wondered how he had missed that the whole time she had been standing there. "Can I sleep on your floor?"

"Yeah, of course, come on in."

Eli closed the door behind her. He went to the bed and began removing the pillow and blanket from it.

"You're not sleeping on the ground, though. Take the bed."

"Are you sure?"

"Yeah, I'm good down here," Eli set up a spot for himself on the floor.

"Okay," she replied, unsurely.

"I promise, it's fine." He laid down on his makeshift bed. "Night."

"Night."

Lucy got into the bed and turned off the light. Eli stared at the ceiling, trying to steady his breathing as he listened to hers. It wasn't the uncomfortable ground that was keeping him awake, more so that his mind was racing. He thought about Lucy, his kiss with Callie, and not to mention the dangers that still lay ahead. On the one hand, he felt like he shouldn't be thinking about girls when his circumstances were this dire. But, if these were possibly his last days, shouldn't he be trying to enjoy them?

"Are you still awake?" Lucy's whisper interrupted his internal battle.

"Couldn't say no if I wasn't."

"Will you just share the bed?"

"What?" Eli puzzled, "That's not why I can't sleep, Lucy. I'm fine down here."

"Well, it's why I can't sleep. I feel guilty about you being on the floor and I am too tired to be feeling anything. Please, just share the bed with me. I promise I'll stay on my side."

Eli hesitated. It wasn't her staying away that concerned him, but he obliged. He picked up his bedding and laid down next to her, making sure he stayed as close to the edge of his side as possible.

"Hey, Eli?"

"Yeah?"

"It's okay to be scared." Lucy's voice was barely above a whisper. Eli shifted onto his side, and Lucy shifted as well, both of them facing each other. "You're not alone in that. But, as long as we all stick together, we're gonna be fine."

"Thanks."

If only she knew what was actually scaring him at that moment. As if he somehow lost control of his limbs, Eli felt his hand reach out and push a lock of Lucy's hair out of her face. He held his breath, wondering if that was okay. Lucy responded by snuggling closer to him, her head now merely inches from his.

"Still scared?" She asked, coyly.

"Terrified." Eli exhaled. Lucy moved her head closer, her lips nearly brushing against his, and just as quickly pulled her head away. She rolled onto her back once more, chuckling.

"Good night, Waldo."

Eli couldn't help but grin. He rolled back over as well, still feeling the sensation on his lips. He had been right. The kiss with Callie was nothing compared to the things Lucy could make him feel. Maybe one day, he'd be able to tell her that. For now, though, he just closed his eyes and drifted off to sleep.

Chapter Twelve

Apollo sat in a darkened holding room just outside of the gates to Tartarus. The walls surrounding him held large glass cases with mighty fires blazing inside. The god looked up to the ceiling, sighing in discontent.

"Apollo." A large man entered the room. "I never thought that you would have been the first one arrested. I always assumed it would be Dionysus if I'm being honest."

"Yes, well, a hoplite got in a lucky shot while my back was turned, Hades. Not much I could do about that." Apollo replied, eyeing the man, before rising.

Hades gave a slow smile, and both gods laughed, sharing an embrace, and patting each other on the back.

"Honestly," Hades chuckled. "This was Zeus' plan? To send you all to me?"

"I think he thought Ares would be smart enough to make sure I actually made it into the prison."

"My brother is an idiot."

"Here, here." Apollo smiled. "Can you get me back to the hotel? My powers don't work here."

"Of course, Apollo." Hades held up his hand, fingers prepared in a snapping pose. "Oh, before I forget, you have a visitor there. I don't believe she knew you weren't home."

"She?"

With a grin, Hades snapped his fingers together and Apollo was standing alone at the door to his suite. Cautiously, he pushed the door open, stepping inside and finding the woman seated on his couch. He sucked in a breath as he saw her.

"Calliope."

The woman's eyes narrowed. "You know I hate that name."

"Sorry." Apollo held up his hands in surrender. "I forgot you go by Callie now."

"Easy to forget when it's been so long." She said, sadly. "Anyway, I came by to let you know your Five are safe. I just left them having the time of their lives at Nectar."

Apollo walked over to the kitchen and poured himself a glass of water.

"I've had a really long night, Callie. Please, just get to the point of your visit. I'm sure the 'Chief of all Muses' has better places to be."

"Charming, as always." She rolled her eyes, standing up and walking over to join Apollo. "I genuinely just wanted to let you know. I know how important their mission is to you."

"Okay, great. Then you've let me know." He raised his glass to her and took a sip. "You can leave now."

"It doesn't have to be like this, Apollo." Callie glared.

"You left me." Apollo slammed the glass down on the counter, causing small cracks to form. "I loved you, and you left me. Now you come back a hundred years later, just to give me a status update? I don't know how else you expected it to be."

He took a deep breath, regained his composure, and walked into the living room. He sat down on the sofa and leaned his head back, closing his eyes in frustration. Callie remained at the counter, tears in her eyes.

"I left you." She whispered. "I never stopped loving you."

When Apollo looked back, Callie was gone.

"Well. That was uncomfortable."

Apollo whipped his head around to find Dionysus leaning against the doorway to the hall.

"How long have you been there?"
"Long enough to know it was uncomfortable." The younger god walked over and plopped down on the couch across from Apollo, laying in a reclined position. "Why'd you yell at her, anyway? You know she's your one true love."
"Oh, shut up, you have no clue what you're talking about."
"I was there, man. I saw you two together in your prime. Who cares if she had other stuff to do?"
"Other stuff?" Apollo exclaimed. "She married another guy!"
"Eh, I still think you're overreacting."

Apollo grabbed a throw pillow and whipped it at Dionysus' face.

Chapter Thirteen

The alarm clock startled Eli awake at 7:15 am on the dot. He reached over and smacked it a few times before it finally turned off. His head was pounding as he remembered the events of the night before. It seemed hazy now, but the parts he remembered made him feel sick. That could just be the hangover, though, he realized.

As he looked down, he saw that during the night, Lucy's head had ended up on his chest, an arm wrapped around his torso. Eli couldn't help but smile. He brushed a few stray hairs out of her face, admiring how peaceful she looked. It almost felt criminal to wake her up when she looked this way. Even her loud snoring was cute somehow.

"Hey," Eli's voice was hoarse, so he cleared his throat and tried again. "Hey, Lucy, it's time to wake up."

Lucy grumbled something and opened her eyes, noticing the position she was in. She jumped away from Eli.

"Oh. Sorry, I don't know how I—"
"Trust me, it's okay," Eli laughed.
"Well, either way,' she smiled, "my bad. Thank you

for letting me crash in here. I'm just gonna head back to my room now and I'll see you at Theo's in a bit?"

"Yeah, see you soon," Eli nodded.

After the door closed behind her, Eli got dressed and sat on his bed for a moment with his head in his hands. Now that he had sobered up, guilt washed over him. He knew he had no reason to feel guilty, not technically. He and Lucy weren't together or anything. But something inside him felt awful. As if he had cheated on her somehow.

Eli shook off his nerves and got up to grab his bag. He slung the duffel over his shoulder and headed to Theo's.

"Good morning, sunshine!" Theo answered the door with a grin. Eli could not and would never understand how he could be so chipper so early in the morning. Especially after how many drinks they had the night before.

He realized he was the first one there and cursed himself for not sleeping in an extra ten minutes. As he inhaled the scent of fresh coffee brewing, however, his spirits lifted. Lucy must've brought it on her way to his room last night, he thought. He walked inside, put his bag down next to Theo's bed, and headed straight for the urn.

By the time his coffee was done, the others had arrived. Wyatt looked as bad as Eli felt. Liv didn't seem too pleasant either and Eli wondered if something happened after the boys got back last night. Lucy looked beautiful, as always.

The three made themselves a cup of coffee as well and went to sit on the bed, laying the map out on the bedspread.

"So, I was looking over the map last night," Wyatt began.

"Last night?" Eli blurted out in surprise. Lucy furrowed her brows at his question.

"Okay, fine, it was this morning, Waldo. Ya happy now?" Wyatt glared as Liv rolled her eyes. "Anyway, it looks like we're gonna have to head back south before we can go east again. It should only add an extra 20 minutes, give or take."

"That's not too bad," Eli said, taking a sip from his cup. "So, we can finish our coffee and plan to leave by 8:30?"

"That's what I was—" A knock on the door interrupted Wyatt's thought. "That's probably housekeeping."

"We're okay in here," Theo called out, politely. "Thank you, anyway."

The knocking continued, becoming louder with every rap. Liv gave a frustrated sigh, and marched over to the door, swinging it open.

"We said—" her shriek cut through her words.

Standing in front of Liv was a shirtless man with no head. His face was literally in his chest, with black eyes and sharp fang-like teeth. Liv slammed the door back shut and pushed against it.

"Anthropophage!" Wyatt gasped.

Eli's heart nearly leaped out of his chest. "What's that? Is it bad? It sounds bad."

"Cannibals." He answered, grabbing his bow and arrows. "And who do you think sent them?"

Zeus. Eli's chest tightened. Theo darted forward to help Liv hold off the beast while Eli drew his sword. Lucy ran to the bathroom door, placing her hand as soon as she got there.

"How did he find us?!"

"How do you think, Eli?" Wyatt's eyes flashed.

Oh, gods. Was it Callie? Eli looked over at Lucy but luckily, she wasn't paying attention to their conversation. He didn't believe that Callie would've sold them out, but he knew nothing about her. Eli placed his hand to his temple. What if she was working with Zeus? How could he be so stupid?

The hotel door swung open, and Liv and Theo flew backward. Eli heard a loud cracking sound. Theo jumped to his feet, but Liv stayed on the ground.

"Liv!" Wyatt cried. He nocked an arrow and sent it flying towards the cannibal, hitting him in the leg. The creature roared in pain, taking a step back. Wyatt took the opportunity and rushed forward, he and Theo both picking Liv up and helping her limp to the portal.

Eli took a few swings and pushed the beast back outside the door. He slammed the door once more and ran into the portal as well. Lucy shut a fire exit door behind them, and they looked around to find themselves in the hotel parking lot. Eli looked up just in time to see four more of them come around the corner, heading straight for the Five.

"Looks like they travel in packs." Eli pointed towards the monsters. "We've gotta go, now."

The group took off in a sprint, following the golden path.

"That's so wild that anthropophage are chasing us," Wyatt panted as he ran. "Did you guys know the last sighting of one was hundreds of years ago?"

"When?" Lucy replied, breathing heavily

"Not since the 1500s!"

"No, when did we ask?" Wyatt stuck his tongue out at her as they continued to run.

About a mile later, Eli noticed a sign for a train station up ahead.

"Guys, follow me. We can try to lose them in there."

The group agreed, trailing behind him. Eli led them into the station, jumping over the turnstiles that guarded the platforms. He looked back to see the Cannibals were still right on their tails. Eli groaned inwardly, disappointed that they hadn't shaken them. Once they made it onto an empty platform, Eli stopped them.

"We can't outrun them. We're gonna have to kill them." He stated, breathing hard.

"Can we try to reason with them?" Lucy wheezed, placing her hands on her knees. "Maybe they hate Zeus as much as we do."

"Anthropophage only speak one language. It's their own, and it's specific to them. No one else in the world knows it." Wyatt frowned. "I think Eli's right. This is just like a trial. If we can't fight them, we have no shot at fighting Zeus."

"Agreed." Liv went to draw her sword and limped over to them, her face red and distorted in pain. Only then did Eli realize that the cracking sound he heard in the hotel room must have been one of her bones fracturing.

"Hold on," Eli quickly went to her and put his hands on her leg, healing her broken bone.

He made an extra effort not to look at her leg for too long and avoided Wyatt's gaze as he healed. Moments later, she stood up straight, wiping the tears from her face and taking a warrior's stance.

Eli unsheathed his sword as well, and Lucy held up her fists. Theo closed his eyes tightly and grimaced as his bones cracked. His body twisted forward and seconds later, a humongous wolf stood in his place.

Wyatt raised his bow and knocked an arrow, patiently aiming towards the entrance. Liv and Eli both drew their swords, and Lucy crouched slightly as if entering a fighter's pose.

The Cannibals made it up onto the platform as well and Wyatt released his arrow, hitting the center anthropophage in his leg. The creature let out a guttural shriek, and all Hell broke loose.

With the arrow still sticking out of his knee, the beast headed straight for Wyatt, while the others split off. Wyatt dinged it with his arrows three more times before it got close enough to swing, now resembling a terrifying pin cushion. Wyatt dropped his bow to fight with his bare hands. He swung on the Cannibal and missed as the beast dodged his attacks. As the creature's head came back up, it dove forward, sinking its teeth into Wyatt's arm. Wyatt reached over and grabbed an arrow that was stuck in the monster's arm. With all of his force, he stabbed the arrow into its face. It let go immediately and dropped to the ground, a dark purple liquid gushing out from its teeth.

"Go for the face- er, the chest. Oh, you know what I mean." He exclaimed to the others.

The anthropophage attacking Liv grabbed her arm and shoved her face-first into the guardrail. Liv staggered back, having trouble finding her footing. Wyatt ran up behind her and steadied her. Once she was back up straight, she faced the beast head-on. With blood streaming from her nose and anger in her eyes, she screamed and sliced the beast's torso clean off its body.

Wolf Theo growled and nipped at the one closest to him. The creature kicked at him, jamming its heel into the wolf's face. He whimpered and turned away for a moment, panting hard. Narrowing his eyes, Wolf Theo jumped up at the anthropophage, biting it squarely in the shoulder, and bringing it to its knees. Liv ran over and drove her sword through the beast, twisting it until he fell limp.

Lucy picked up the largest one by the neck and slammed him down to the ground, cracking the surrounding cement. While she held him there, Eli raised his sword. The creature grabbed Lucy's arm and twisted himself free. Lucy yelped in pain and jumped backward, landing on the ground at its feet. The monster stomped toward her, letting out a ferocious roar that was so powerful it blew her hair backward. The creature lifted its hand to strike, and Eli lunged forward, driving his sword through the beast's back until the tip of the blade came out of its face.

Eli pulled the sword back out and sheathed it as the anthropophage toppled to the ground. His stomach churned and before he knew it, he was kneeling over the side of the platform, throwing up onto the tracks. He felt a hand on his back and turned to see Theo had reemerged as a human. Eli nodded his appreciation to him and stood back up. As the Five surveyed the damage, Eli healed Lucy and Theo up while Wyatt helped Liv clean the blood off of her face, all of them silent save for their heavy breathing. Suddenly, in the distance, they could hear a train horn fast approaching.

"We've gotta get out of here." Theo insisted, quietly.
"Do we—" Lucy cleared her throat. "Do we just leave them here?"

"The gods' magic will take care of them," Wyatt answered. "Mortal blood can't see mythological monsters. They should disappear at any moment, but for now, Theo's right. Mortals can still see us, so we need to go now."

Lucy nodded, and they all departed the platform quickly.

Chapter Fourteen

After they put a few more miles between themselves and the corpses, they finally slowed down to rest in the forest off of the main road. Eli finished healing Wyatt and Liv while Lucy reached into her portal bags and grabbed sandwiches and water for everyone.

"I know we're on a time crunch," Lucy began. "But should we just camp here for the night?"

"I know you're tired, Lu, we all are," Theo sympathized, "but we have to put at least a little more distance between us and those things we left behind."

"Fine," she sighed. "Let's get going then. Sooner we get there, sooner I can sleep."

The group trekked on for about six more hours, stopping only for bathroom and snack breaks. Once they made it into Sitirio, they finally stopped and made camp. The woods they were in were thick, filled with lush green foliage that surrounded them. Eli could hear songbirds singing high above them in the trees, and a light breeze whipped around him. He was grateful, as the heat from the sun had been torturing him the entire way there.

The group had brought along two tents, which were not very large. Liv pouted, but Wyatt argued to her that they were such small tents that it would be uncomfortable for Lucy to have to share with Theo and Eli. Finally, she conceded, and they decided the girls would share one while the boys shared the other.

"I'm wired anyway, so I'm gonna stay up and keep watch, just in case." Theo offered.

"You need rest too, though." Wyatt reasoned. "Give me four hours of sleep and I'll take the second shift."

"Okay, that works," Theo agreed.

After dinner, Lucy and Eli sat on a log by the fire. Liv and Wyatt were arguing in hushed tones near the tents, and Theo shifted into a hawk to watch over them from the treetops above.

"What do you think they're arguing about?" Lucy asked, gesturing at Wyatt and Liv.

"Your guess is as good as mine," Eli answered. "Maybe she's still just upset over the sleeping arrangements."

"Maybe." Lucy frowned. "It seems like she's been upset with him since this morning, though. Do you think they got into a fight last night?"

"It's really none of our business. They'll work it out, I'm sure." Eli felt bad for omitting what he knew.

Surely, the fight was about how drunk Wyatt was the night before. Liv may even have wondered if he had cheated on her at the bar. But if Eli told Lucy about his theories now, she would wonder why he hadn't said something before. If she did that, Eli didn't trust that he wouldn't tell her the truth about Callie, too, and he had a strong feeling that he didn't want to do that. Especially if it turned out that him being so open with Callie was the reason for the attack that morning.

Luckily for him the issue seemed to be solved, as Wyatt pulled Liv in for a kiss.

"See?" Eli nudged Lucy. "They always work it out."

"I guess you're right. Well, I'll see you in the morning, Waldo." Lucy nodded to him, before turning to Liv. "Hey lover girl, are you coming to bed?"

Liv broke apart from Wyatt and giggled. "That sounded dirty."

Lucy grinned in response. "Good, that's what I was going for."

■■

It was midafternoon when the Five finally made it to Elitsa. The sun was high and the light reflecting off of the cool blue waves was an enchanting sight. Hills upon hills of blue and white homes overlooked the ocean.

The city was larger than Eli had imagined it as the group made their way to the docks. Eli was on edge with every person they passed. He knew logically that they were probably only staring because they were five strangers, but his paranoia after the Anthropophage attack had him looking over his shoulder at every turn.

Once the group finally made it to the docks, Eli could relax for a moment, as they were seemingly the only ones there. The smell of the salt from the sea was calming, and he took a deep breath in.

"I'm not sure why, but I thought there would be a pirate ship." Liv mused.

"That makes no sense," Lucy tilted her head, "but also, I agree."

"I don't think any of these are charters." Theo's voice sounded troubled.

Looking around, Eli had to agree. A range of small to large boats lined the docks, all of which looked like they were privately owned.

"Also, are we even sure we can take a boat?" Eli wondered. "The path wouldn't let us take a car."

"You think the universe expects us to swim the whole way?" Wyatt asked condescendingly.

"It expected us to walk the whole way." Eli retorted.

He felt slightly proud of himself that he was getting better at dealing with Wyatt's attitude. Seeing him nearly fall over drunk had given Eli a bit more courage to stand up to him.

"Well, let's just find a boat and we can figure it out." Theo stepped in between them.

"Surely, there is someone around here to take people out on boat rides." Wyatt looked around, squinting, and held his hand over his eyes to block out the sun. "It's the Aegean Sea, for crying out loud. You would think it's a tourist's heaven."

"There's a man by that boat over there." Liv pointed at a sailboat in the distance. "Why don't we just ask him to take us?"

"Uh," Lucy began, skeptically, "because normal people don't just take five foreign strangers on a cruise?"

"Give me five minutes, and everyone, look that way." She smirked, pointing behind them.

Liv reached into her bag and pulled out a silver belt covered in various gemstones and began wrapping it around her waist. The rest of them adhered to her instructions and turned around before she had completely fastened it.

"I'll be right back." She called from behind them.

They each waited patiently, except for Wyatt, who was kicking at the wooden planks with his shoe.

"You know we need a boat, bro," Theo consoled him. "She's gonna be okay."

"I get that, but it still sucks."

"Seriously?" Lucy scoffed and turned to Wyatt. "You can't deal with her talking to another guy for five minutes?"

"Lucy," Theo warned.

"I get that you're in love, I do. I even get that she can be flighty and flirty. But what she's doing right now is literally to save the world. You would think the group genius would get that."

"Lucy!" This time, Theo's voice was more assertive, causing Lucy to snap her mouth shut.

"Do you actually know what can happen to the wearer of that belt? In some cases, the men don't just fall in love, they become obsessed. So, I'm not going to apologize for being concerned." Wyatt glared. "And even if I was jealous, feelings aren't something that can be controlled, Lucy. You would know that if you ever felt anything at all."

Lucy recoiled as if he had slapped her. Eli felt a wave of anger rise inside of him.

"Wyatt, back off."

"Or what, Waldo?" Wyatt puffed out his chest. "She gets to say rude things to me all the time, but it's okay, right? Because she's just joking?"

"It's not okay at all. You are right, and she's right, too. What's not right is the way you're both treating each other." Eli looked from Wyatt to Lucy, his brows raised. "We have actual monsters coming at us from all sides. The only way we're going to get through this is together."

"But—"

"No, Lucy. I know you were just saying how you felt, but you overstepped, and you were really harsh."

Wyatt grunted in agreement.

"And you," Eli turned his attention back to Wyatt, "you have every right to feel the way you feel. No one knows a relationship better than the person in it. But what you said to Lucy was cold. Both of you need to apologize right now."

"Sorry," Lucy and Wyatt muttered in unison.

"Honestly," Eli continued. "Do you guys even realize that the only reason you two fight so much is because you're the same person?"

"We are not!" Lucy looked offended.

"Defensive, cocky, and abrasive. Not to mention stubborn."

"I agree with you, Eli." Wyatt nodded. "That sounds exactly like her."

Lucy reached up and smacked Wyatt on the back of the head. Eli looked over at Theo and pulled his lips into a thin line to keep from laughing.

"Ow!" Wyatt's hand flew to where she had hit him, but they were both laughing now as well.

"Alright, guys, the belt's off." Liv's voice called out from behind them as she walked back to them. Her face twisted in amusement once they all turned around. "Did I miss something?"

"Nah, just Eli being a good momma bear." Theo jested.

"Uh, okay," Liv replied, perplexed. "Well, anyway, I've got the keys. Are we ready to go?"

"Yeah." Wyatt smiled at her. "One quick question. Does anyone here actually know how to sail a sailboat?"

"I've seen every Pirates of the Caribbean movie," Lucy remarked. "It can't be that hard."

Chapter Fifteen

"I was wrong!" Lucy yelled from the front of the boat; her legs tangled in thick ropes. "This is very hard!"

Once they were aboard the boat, they found the path remained visible to them. Eli didn't understand why, and he hated the smug look on Wyatt's face, but he was grateful that they would not have to swim.

"I found a manual below deck," Theo called to Lucy, trying to shout over the wind. "We have to start by setting the mainsail. The line to the boom must be well eased, so the sail spills luffs and doesn't fill prematurely."
"I understood some of those words. The 'prematurely' thing isn't a big deal, no matter what anyone says. With time and practice, you'll get better."

Liv, Wyatt, and Eli all dissolved into giggles.

"That's not what I said!"
"What?" she shouted.
"I said, that's not what I— Oh, forget it."
"Set it? What should I be setting?"
"Lucy, just come back." Eli laughed and waved her over.

Once Lucy was free from the tangles, she made her way back to the others.

"So, none of us know how to sail," Wyatt stated.

"Now what do we do?" Theo asked.

Lucy smacked herself in the forehead. "My gods, we're dumb. Liv."

"Hm?" Liv looked up at her.

"Of course," Wyatt nodded. "Liv, we can't drive the boat. But you can move the sea under us."

Liv's eyes widened, and she gasped.

"Well, would you look at me?" She grinned proudly. "I'm being so useful today."

She stood up and moved her hands in a wave motion, up and down rhythmically. Eli thought to himself that, if they made it out of this alive, she should look into hula dancing. Her form was fantastic.

The boat slowly started moving towards their destination, the golden path rippling in front of them with the waves. After a few moments, they picked up speed, and the Five let out a cheer.

"Hell yes!" Lucy exclaimed.

"Do you have to do that the whole time, though?" Eli asked Liv, motioning to her hands.

"If we want to keep moving, yeah. I can at least keep it up for a few more hours, though."

"That works," Wyatt confirmed. "We can drop anchor when you can't move us anymore. That way, we can all eat dinner and set up for bed."

Below the deck, there were three rooms. Theo and Eli decided they would bunk together, leaving one room for

Lucy and one for Liv and Wyatt to share. Liv got excited when she heard that plan and the boat moved even faster forward.

Lucy sat with Liv to keep her company, while the boys found fishing poles and took a crack at catching dinner. By the time Liv started getting tired, the sun had already set. The boys caught nothing, realizing afterward it probably wasn't a good idea to try fishing while they were moving.

Lucy, instead, searched through the portal in her bag to find food from the penthouse. As they all sat around eating dinner and laughing, Eli felt something stir inside of him. If he didn't know any better, he would think they were all just on vacation. No battles to be fought, no gods to defeat. Just friends, eating food, and having fun with each other. At that moment, Eli couldn't imagine anything better.

• •

"Help!"

"Did you hear that?" Theo whispered in the dark, moonlight shining across his face through the porthole in their cabin.

"Hear what?" Eli answered sleepily. He looked over at the clock and yawned. They had only been asleep for three hours.

"It sounded like a woman's voice."

"It's probably just Liv or Lucy."

"No, it was someone different." Theo reached over and turned on the light.

Eli squinted his eyes, groaning and pulling his pillow over his face.

"We're on a boat in the middle of the sea, you maniac," Eli grumbled, his voice slightly muffled. "There's no strange woman's voice here. Let me sleep."
"Okay," Theo replied. "You're right. Sorry."

Theo reached back up and turned the light off again. Eli placed his pillow back under his head and settled in.

"Help me!"

Both boys sat straight up.

"Okay, I heard it that time," Eli admitted, getting out of bed.

Theo jumped out of bed and joined him, both boys scrambling to get dressed. Eli grabbed his sword, and the pair ran out onto the top deck, where they found Wyatt and Liv.

"Did you hear the voice?" Theo asked.
Wyatt nodded. "Liv thought I was going crazy."
"Can you not hear it?" Theo turned to Liv.
"No, but I'm a bit more worried now knowing both of you can."
"Did you see anyone out there?" Eli asked, his voice concerned. He looked around but saw no one else.
"No, it's like it was a dream," Wyatt replied.
"Help!"

The boys split up, each running to a different side of the vessel, searching for where the voice was coming from. Just then, Lucy appeared from below deck, shuffling over to Eli.

"What's going on?"

"Lucy can't hear it either?" Wyatt called out.

"Hear what?" Lucy asked.

"We can't find her." Eli peered out over the sea.

"Find who?" Her voice was getting more and more irritated. "Will someone please tell me what the hell is happening?"

"They're hearing a woman's voice, calling for help." Liv filled her in.

"In the middle of the Aegean Sea?" Lucy's eyebrows narrowed and then her face went calm. "In the middle of the Aegean Sea. Hey Liv, why don't you come and help me look over here?"

Eli kept searching, frightened for the woman that he was sure was drowning somewhere out at sea. So frightened in fact, that he did not notice where Lucy and Liv went. He also did not notice them talking in hushed tones, grabbing heaps of rope from the bow of the ship. And he definitely did not notice the pair knocking out Wyatt and Theo, tying them to the mast. He felt a hand on his shoulder, however, as Lucy spun him around. She lifted her fist, and everything went black.

∙∙

Eli found it difficult to open his eyes. His head was pounding, and he was pretty sure he had gone deaf. He finally squeezed one eye open enough to see why. He was bound to the mast of the ship. Wyatt and Theo were tied up next to him as well, fast asleep. Even though he could see Liv and Lucy talking, he couldn't hear a word they were saying.

"What's going on?" He heard his voice in his head, but out of his mouth, it sounded muffled, as if he was speaking into a pillow.

Lucy looked over, mouthed something to Liv, and marched toward him. Once she was within inches, she reached over to him and plucked something out of his ear.

"Morning, sunshine." She smiled. Eli could hear the faint sounds of a woman humming from all around them. *Where is she?*

"What did you do?"
"Nothing much. Just saved your asses, that's all."
"What—"
"You guys really hear a strange woman's voice in the middle of the sea, while we're on an epic Greek journey, and never once think to yourself, 'Hmm. Maybe it's a Siren.' I swear." She rolled her eyes. "Liv and I rounded you guys up and stuck cotton balls in your ears. If you can't hear them, you won't whine about us killing them."
"You're crazy." Eli spat. "You can't kill her. I love her!"
"Yeah, okay, and this is where the cotton comes in." Lucy stuck the ball back in his ear, but Eli's panic did not subside.

He looked over to the side of the ship and suddenly she appeared, a vision before Eli's eyes. She looked like a beautiful woman from the waist up. From the bottom down, a bird. She had large, gorgeous white wings protruding from her back like an angel. Eli struggled against the ropes, crying out in anguish.

As he cried, the girls took notice of the Siren. They took a step back, readying themselves. Liv drew her sword, mouthed something to Lucy, and attacked. Eli whimpered but couldn't look away, as they tossed about his one true love and slashed her to pieces right in front of his eyes.

It was only when Liv struck the final blow that he let out the breath he didn't realize he had been holding in. His cheeks were wet, and he could still feel how much his heart had hurt, but more than that, he felt embarrassed. He felt the ropes around him wiggle and looked over to see Wyatt and Eli had awoken. They, too, seemed distraught at what they had just witnessed.

The girls walked over to them and removed the cotton from each of their ears.

"How are we feeling?" Liv smirked at them.
"Please don't kill her." Theo cried out in response.

Liv and Lucy looked at each other in confusion.

"The spell should have broken." Said Lucy.

Caws and screeches sounded out from all around them. Three more Sirens flew up and landed on deck. The three boys stood mesmerized by their beauty.

"I'm guessing they have something to do with it," Liv replied, readying her sword once more.

Suddenly, the ropes gave way. Eli looked over at Theo, who had shifted into a massive hawk to escape the ropes. He flew high above them, then nose-dived, headed straight for Lucy and Liv.

"I don't want to hurt you, Theo, but I will." Lucy swatted at him while Liv took on the Sirens.

With the ropes now looser, Eli and Wyatt untangled themselves. Wyatt ran over to Liv and tackled her. Liv presented him with an elbow to the nose in response.

Eli stood, thinking. The girls were going to kill the Sirens, and he couldn't let that happen, but his sword was across the deck, past the fighting. He had no way to run to it, so he tried to join Theo to attack from the skies. He squeezed his eyes and became the size of a bird. No matter how hard he flapped his wings, however, he could not fly.

A chicken? Again?! This was just getting ridiculous now. Eli squawked in frustration. There was no time to change back, so he did the only thing he knew to do. He ran at Lucy and pecked her on the legs as hard as he could.

"Ow!" Lucy looked down to see what was biting her and narrowed her eyes at what she saw. "You've got to be fucking kidding me"

Lucy kicked Eli so hard that he flew off the boat, landing in the water with a small plop. He focused all of his energy on shifting back, finally feeling his human form return as he floated into the sea.

The water was freezing, the salty taste forcing its way down Eli's throat. He kicked his feet frantically, clawing at the waves to get back to the boat, but it was no use. The current was too strong, and he tired quickly. Just then, he heard the voice again. A gorgeous melody was being sung from beneath the waves.

Eli took a deep breath and forced his head under the surface. He looked deeper and saw the Siren floating gracefully as if dancing to the ebb and flow of the water. Eli dove farther into the temperamental sea to reach her. He could feel his lungs ache, but he did not care. All he knew was that he needed to be with her. His vision blurred, and his head felt woozy. Before he could react, he coughed, his lungs filling with water. The last thing Eli saw before passing out was the heavenly glow of green light reflecting off of the moon and onto the Siren's face.

Chapter Sixteen

Eli awoke, still under the water, but now able to breathe. He coughed and gasped for air, disoriented, and trying to understand his surroundings.

A large bubble seemed to surround him, an invisible air pocket deep under the waves. Though he was no longer submerged in water, he still floated, his feet unable to find the bottom of the bubble. Eli wondered if that was a good thing.

"Surely, if I touch the bubble, it will pop." He mused aloud to himself, his voice echoing around him. He realized at that moment that he no longer had the urge to find the Siren and sighed in relief.

To his left, he saw an enormous shadow moving through the sea. The shadow floated horizontally along the shape of the bubble's walls.

"Sup, little dude!" A man who looked to be in his 30s crossed into the air pocket, shaking excess water out of his long white hair.

He was holding a large, golden trident in one hand. In the other was something that looked an awful lot to Eli, like a pipe for tobacco.

"I was totally buggin', man. I thought they wasted you for sure." The man floated closer to Eli.

"I drowned," Eli said uneasily, filling with panic at the realization of his situation. "Are you Charon? Am I dead? I don't remember anyone mentioning him as having a trident. Would I even remember? Is that why I'm floating?"

"Whoa, whoa, whoa, little dude. You have got to chill out. Seaweed?" The man offered the pipe to Eli, who shook his head in return. "Suit yourself, friend. At least take a deep breath with me. Inhale," he breathed in deeply, waiting for Eli to do the same.

After a moment, Eli joined him, exhaling slowly.

"Good job, little buddy! The name's Poseidon. Pleasure to meet ya."

Eli thought he would've been used to meeting the gods by now, but he still felt himself getting nervous, somehow sweating through his already drenched clothes.

"I'm um, Eli," he finally eked out, swallowing hard.

"Well, Um Eli," Poseidon grinned brightly, "what brings you to my neck of the woods? Besides chasing tail, that is."

Eli looked at him in confusion. "Chasing? No. I was under a spell, I didn't—"

"Yeah, chasing that Siren to your death, dude. Look, I get it, dating inside your own species can be wicked hard. But you can't just go trying to bang a Siren, man."

"Hey, I wasn't trying to!" Eli became frustrated. He looked at the god's face and saw the beginning of a smile forming. "Oh, you're messing with me."

"Sorry, dude, it's really easy," Poseidon confirmed, laughing.

He floated closer to Eli and mimed sitting on a chair. He patted the air next to him, offering Eli an invisible seat as well.

"Now, seriously, but not too seriously, tell me what brings you here."

Eli floated over and mimed a seat as well, crossing his legs as if to meditate mid-air.

"My friends and I are just out sailing. Exploring, actually." Eli was hesitant to reveal anything, not knowing if Poseidon was on Zeus' side or not. "We just stopped for the night when the sirens attacked. Where did they go, by the way?"

"Your friends took care of the ones above. Those dudettes of yours are scrappy as hell, my guy. If you decide you don't like fish, I'd give one of them a shot, for sure."

Eli felt his face redden at the mere mention of Lucy, and the god's follow-up on the subject didn't make it any better.

"The one down here," Poseidon continued, "got fed to my favorite Thresher Shark, Chad."

"You have a pet shark named Chad?" Eli chuckled.

"Hell yeah, I do. He may not be man's best friend, but he's mine for sure." Poseidon replied. "Anyway, once you passed out, I popped you in here. Breathing underwater is no bueno for mortals."

"Yeah, I noticed. Well, thank you."

"No problemo. I'm gonna be real with you, Eli. Can I, like, call you Eli?"

Eli furrowed his brows and nodded slowly.

"Righteous." Poseidon continued. "Check it out, five mortals, who can change into chickens, and body slam Sirens, are making their way across the Aegean Sea. I didn't read the prophecy, but even I know what that means, dude."

Eli rose from where he had been 'seated', preparing to find an escape.

"Bro, if I was gonna kill you, I wouldn't have bothered to save you. Think about it, dummy." Poseidon pointed to his temple mockingly. "I'm not on little bro's side here. I'm just also not trying to rile him up. He is not chill at all when he's mad, man. I live by a very simple philosophy down here. No stress, no mess, no fish sex."

Eli snorted at the last bit. "Well then, thank you again. For the colorful philosophy, and for not killing me."

"You are welcome, compadre. Alright, let's get you back to your friends, yeah?" Poseidon rose as well and pointed his trident upwards.

The bubble took off like a bullet towards the surface. Just before it breached the waves, Poseidon shot one last grin at Eli.

"Cowabunga, little dude. Nice meeting you!"

The god disappeared as the bubble flew out of the ocean and through the air towards the boat. It popped Eli back onto the deck of the ship, bursting and spraying water as he landed with a thud.

"What the hell was that?" Lucy asked, wringing out her hair.

Eli looked around at his friends, who were shaking off the seawater that had crashed down upon them. Scattered around the deck were siren corpses and carnage from the battle that had taken place while Eli was with Poseidon. He waited to tell them about his meeting with the god. He was too tired to answer the questions he knew would follow.

"Did we win?" Eli asked.

"No, *we* did," Lucy gestured at herself and Liv. "You guys almost got us all killed."

"Thank you both." Wyatt put his arm around Liv, hugging her close to him. Liv leaned over and kissed him on the nose.

"Really," Eli croaked out, "Thank you, guys. We would've been goners."

"Aw, boys. You really would have." Liv said as she and Lucy both giggled.

Eli fixed his attention on healing everyone's wounds, taking slightly longer with Wyatt's broken nose than necessary.

"You guys need some sleep," Lucy said. "Liv and I had a few hours, and heaps of adrenaline, so we're gonna stay up here. We'll get the boat moving again and keep watch."

The boys nodded in agreement and started back towards their rooms.

"Oh wait, one more thing." Liv held out the cotton balls to each of them. "Better safe than sorry."

Chapter Seventeen

The sun was high in the sky as the Five finally spotted the Isle of Extinction. The island itself seemed small; Eli noted. Tall palm trees lined the beach, and beautifully colored red and blue birds flew overhead. The golden shine of the path seemed to glow brighter the closer that they got.

"Land ho!" Eli cried out from the starboard side, leaning against the ship's railing.

"Yeah, we can all see it," Lucy teased.

"Sorry, I've just always wanted to say that."

Once they were close enough, the group anchored the ship. Theo had read in the manual that if they got too close to the island, they would 'run aground' and have no way to get back to sea. While no one actually understood what that meant, the book made it sound pretty bad, so they decided not to risk it. Liv waved her arms and created a split in the water, forging a path for them to get to the island.

As they walked on the sandy path, Eli watched the clear blue water in awe. They were walking at least twenty feet under the sea and looking at the sides of the water felt like looking at a skyscraper. Colorful fish jumped over their heads from one side to the other, and there were beautiful seashells and pieces of green sea glass strewn about. Through the wall of ripples, gigantic shadows passed by in the distance.

"Did you guys see that turtle? It was huge!" Eli knew he sounded like a little kid at the zoo, but that's how he felt.

A large brown tortoise swam right past them, and four smaller turtles followed close behind.

Wyatt laughed. "It's probably a Stupendemys. They were enormous turtles that died out about ten million years ago."

"If it died out, how is it here?"

"It's called the Isle of Extinction." Lucy offered. "What did you think that meant?"

Eli's face turned red. "I thought it was just a name. Sometimes people just name things."

"That's fair, they do," Wyatt nodded, "but she's right. This island is where extinct things go."

"Wait," Eli stopped in his tracks. "There are a lot of terrifying extinct things, too. What about prehistoric creatures? Are we walking straight into a T-Rex den right now?"

Wyatt turned and walked back to Eli, sighing. "You panic so much. Doesn't it ever get tiring?"

"I am constantly tired of myself if that's what you're asking."

"According to the Underworld library, all the larger, more dangerous extinct animals have already killed each other," Wyatt reassured him. "You can't put that many predators on one island and expect them all to survive. The most we have to worry about are turtles and maybe a desert rat kangaroo, which are adorable, by the way."

"Okay." Eli bit his bottom lip and began walking once

more. He felt a little better at Wyatt's words but kept his hand close to his sword anyway.

■■■

The Five arrived on the island a few moments later. The golden pathway continued into the island's jungle, disappearing through the trees.

"Do you guys wanna rest and eat lunch before we continue?" Wyatt asked them.

"I don't know about everyone else," Theo disclaimed, "but I'm just ready to see where the end of this damn path leads."

"Same," Eli agreed. The girls also nodded their approval.

"Alright, then." Wyatt smiled. "Into the woods we go."

The five trekked through the jungle, Liv and Eli going first with their swords to clear plants out of their way. The air was humid, and Eli's neck was turning red from how many times he had slapped the bugs away.

"We packed everything in the world, but no one thought to bring bug spray?" He kicked some palm fronds out of the pathway.

As he took his next step forward, the front of his foot collided with a giant log, and he fell forward. From his position on the ground, he heard the others chuckle at him and then immediately fall silent.

Eli lifted his head and came face to face with a large creature staring back at him. It reminded him of a turkey, but much bigger, with a long, curved beak. It had blue-gray plumage, a sizeable head, and a tuft of curly feathers high on its rear end.

"A Dodo bird!" Liv gasped from behind him.
"A Dodo bird?" Eli repeated, slowly rising to his feet.

The bird's head tilted back and forth, studying Eli. It let out a small coo and nuzzled its beak against Eli's legs.

Eli chuckled and leaned down, ruffling its feathers. "You're a cutie, huh?"

Lucy and Liv appeared at Eli's side, gushing over their newly found friend.

"Can we keep it, Wyatt? Please?" Liv turned to look back at him, batting her eyelashes.
"Uh, we're kinda on a mission to save the world, babe. I think it'd probably be happier, and safer if we leave it here with its family." Wyatt answered. He and Theo stepped forward to join them.
"What if it doesn't have a family?" Eli wondered, scratching the bird under its chin. "We could keep it with us just until we reach the end of the path, right? There's no harm in that."
"Come on, Waldo, don't get attached," Theo chuckled. "It is really cute, but we've got important things to do."
"How about this?" Lucy intervened. "How about, if we end up defeating Zeus, we can come back and get him? Like, a reward?"

Wyatt and Theo glanced at each other, smirking.

"Fine," Wyatt agreed. "If we win, we can bring the bird home."

Eli and Liv grinned at the agreement. With a few last pets, they said goodbye, and The Five continued along the path.

Another hour passed, and they finally reached the end of the golden trail, stopping at the mouth of an enormous cave. Looking into it felt like staring into a void, a chill emanating from the inside.

"Are we supposed to go in there?" Liv asked, trembling.

"It looks like it." Eli stepped closer to the opening, trying to get a better look. No matter how hard he tried, all he could see was darkness.

"Not tonight, we aren't." Wyatt's bag dropped to the ground with a thud. "I wanna get to the end just as much as you guys, but I think we need a night of rest so that we're better prepared for whatever's in there."

"Okay," Lucy agreed. "Either way, I need to change. You coming, Liv?"

Liv repositioned her bag higher on her shoulder and followed Lucy behind a few palm trees. When Lucy and Liv returned, the boys went to change as well, while the girls pulled out some dinner from the portal bags. When the boys returned, they set up the tents, positioning them farther away from the cave.

As they finished eating, the sun had set. Wyatt used his powers to make a campfire for them, and they all sat in a circle around it. Lucy reached into her bag and pulled out marshmallows, and Eli grabbed long branches from nearby to roast them on. The group sat around, just snacking and telling stories.

Eli felt like they were all thinking the same thing. That tomorrow they would go into the cave, not knowing if all of them would come back out. If they managed to make it out, would they even still be the same people? There were too many unknowns buzzing around them, moving with the mosquitoes and biting them when they least expected it.

■■■

The fire dimmed as Lucy, Theo, and Liv all retreated to their tents. They left Wyatt and Eli alone to make sure the fire went all the way out.

The boys sat in silence, watching the flames dance. The ashes entranced Eli as he watched them dance on the logs, falling into embers underneath. Staring at them, he could imagine the ashes were snowy mountains, atop a bright village that shined from inside, keeping everyone who lived there safe.

The sounds of the jungle swarmed Eli's head as he tried to block out thoughts of the looming dangers that tomorrow would bring.

"You don't have to wait up with me," Wyatt finally said, "if you wanted to go to sleep, I mean."
"Oh, no, I'm fine," Eli replied. "Couldn't sleep right now, anyway."

Wyatt responded with silence, but Eli knew he felt the same.

"If you don't mind me asking, are you and Liv okay?"
"We could be better." Wyatt shrugged. "She didn't like how drunk I was the other night. I told her we were just blowing off steam, and that I was being careful, but she has some unpleasantness from her past regarding alcohol."

"She had been drinking when I first met her, though," Eli said, confused.

"It's not the drinking that's the problem.' Wyatt replied. "It's the amount to which I was drinking. I could barely form a sentence by the time you guys got me back, and I guess that concerned her."

"I get that. You were pretty wasted."

"You're one to talk," Wyatt laughed.

"That's fair." Eli chuckled. "Hey, about the anthropophage…"

"I shouldn't have snapped at you." Wyatt sighed. "We don't know for sure that Callie was the mole. Zeus could've had thousands of other ways to find us."

"Are you sure?" Eli puzzled. "I feel like garbage. I shouldn't have—"

"Had fun? I agree. How dare you?" Wyatt snorted.

"Well, either way." Eli smirked, "thanks for not saying anything."

"No problem. I know you'd do the same for me."

As Wyatt shifted in his seat, Eli heard the jingle from his pocket and remembered something.

"One more thing?"

"The bag that Apollo gave me?" Wyatt read his mind.

Eli nodded in confirmation. He had been curious about it since the journey began but could never find a good time to ask. There were definitely coins in it, but they never really needed money, so Eli couldn't figure out why it was so important.

"Have you ever heard of Charon?" Wyatt asked.

"The Underworld ferryman? Yeah, Lucy told me a little about him when I first got to the penthouse."

"Well, for the ferryman to ferry you, you gotta pay

him. Otherwise, you roam the shores of the Acheron for eternity."

"Okay," Eli sucked in a breath. "So, inside the bag—"

"Inside are five ancient coins called Obols, yes. If someone dies," Wyatt paused, swallowing hard, "then we have to put a coin on or inside their mouth so that they can get back to the Underworld."

Eli's stomach churned, and he felt lightheaded.

"Well then," He rose and stomped out the last of the embers. "I guess we came prepared, after all."

"Let's go get some beauty sleep, Eli." Wyatt stood as well. "Tomorrow's coming, no matter what, so we might as well be gorgeous."

Eli laughed in response and nodded to the boy, both of them heading into the tent they were sharing with Theo. After everything that had happened between them, Eli found himself grateful that Wyatt was there. Who would've thought?

Chapter Eighteen

The opening of the cave was ominous, filling Eli with a sense of dread just from the sight. Wyatt grabbed five flashlights from his bag and distributed them.

"We need to stick together in there," he advised. "If we split up, no one goes off alone."

"Don't have to tell me twice," Lucy's voice shook.

"Ready?" Wyatt looked at his cohorts.

"Ready."

The Five started forward, taking cautious steps. Theo and Liv held their flashlights at the ground, while the others held their beams higher, watching for any dangers they might walk into. On their trek, they side-stepped several large stalagmites. They realized the cave had bats when Wyatt shined his light higher, startling a few awake. They all ducked as the bats screeched and flew at them.

"Turn off your lights and stay as quiet as possible," Theo's voice was barely audible. "If there's a lot of them, we could get really hurt."

The others nodded in agreement, switching off their flashlights as well. In the darkness, Eli saw another light about ten feet in front of them. He nudged Lucy and pointed.

Lucy then nudged Theo to nudge Liv and Wyatt. They each made their way towards it and stopped in awe when they reached it. There was a steep drop into a deeper cavern, filled with water and somehow reflecting shades of blue-green light.

"Do we just jump?" Liv whispered.

Eli looked around, his light landing on a narrow set of stone steps running down the wall.

"I think we just take the stairs," he replied.

Eli went first. Lucy, Theo, and Liv followed, while Wyatt pulled up the rear, watching behind them.

Halfway down, Eli noticed the steps getting slicker. Just as he was about to turn to warn the others, he heard a loud squeak from behind him, followed by Lucy yelping. He turned frantically, in time to see her stumble. He grabbed her arm while Theo steadied her from behind. Once she caught her breath, she nodded to Eli to continue.

Eli waited for the others to join him once he reached the bottom of the steps. A small stream ran through their path, glowing the same blue-green shade they had seen from above. They jumped over it and, looking around their new surroundings, they realized they had reached a dead end.

A large stone wall had caved in, blocking their path. Lucy walked up to the boulders and punched with all of her might. After the impact, she grabbed her hand, screaming out in pain. The rocks did not break, not even a chip. Eli stepped over to her, inspecting her injury.

"I'm no doctor," he whispered, "but it's broken."

"Can you just fix it, please?" Tears streamed down her face.

Eli cradled his hand over hers. He focused with all of his strength, waiting. Lucy cried out again, yanking her hand away.

"Why isn't it working?" Eli wondered. He shook his hand out, frustrated.

"Guys," Theo spoke up, "I can't shape shift either. Something about this place is suppressing our powers."

"Wonderful assessment." A woman's voice echoed throughout the cavern.

Eli pushed Lucy behind him, readying his sword. From the shadows, she appeared. The woman was tall, and beautiful, with a solemn look on her face. She stepped closer to the Five. Eli glanced at the others and noticed Wyatt's eyes widened in shock.

"What is it?" he asked. "Do you know her?"

Wyatt swallowed hard before dropping his weapon and bowing. When he spoke her name aloud, Eli felt chills shoot up his back.

"Athena."

■■

Theo and Liv, dropping her sword, bowed as well. Eli stayed standing and ready, Lucy still behind him.

Wyatt hissed at him, "Show some respect."

"That's quite alright, Wyatt," Athena's face did not show any signs of emotion, but her tone was understanding. "You may all stand."

The three arose to their feet once more.

"What are you doing here? How did you know where we would be?" Eli had many more questions but figured those would be best to figure out if they were in danger or not.

"Elias, I am not here to hurt you. I am here to help you." The goddess stepped forward once more, to which Eli took a step backward in return.

Athena's eyes narrowed. She waved her hand and Eli heard a loud cracking, followed by a sigh of relief from Lucy. He turned to her, checking on her hand and seeing it completely healed.

"Okay," Eli sheathed his sword, "We're listening."

"With the manner in which you are speaking to me, I fear that you have spent too much time with my siblings." She replied. "While I am here to help, please do not think me your peer. I have the power to end worlds. I would not hesitate to end anyone who disrespects me."

Eli swallowed hard. "I apologize."

"Noted. As for your request, I will explain. Centuries ago, I was with Demeter when she got Ales' letter. Once the prophecy left her lips, she turned to me and gave me a mission. I spent the next fifty years searching for this island, and since I arrived, I have never left. I was told I must be here to guide each of you through forging the weapon. It is not as simple as you may believe."

"None of this adventure has been," Theo acknowledged.

"I am sorry to hear that." Athena continued. "I am even sorrier to tell you it does not get easier from here. To forge the weapon, I must spill your blood. Literally and metaphorically."

"What does metaphorically mean?" Liv inquired.

"A metaphor is a figure of speech," Wyatt whispered to her.

"No, I know that." Her cheeks grew red, and she addressed Athena once more. "I was asking, what did you mean that the blood has to be spilled metaphorically?"

"I need drops of your actual blood, and I also need a pain held inside of it." Athena clarified. "It would be akin to the darkest moment in your life. A moment that brought you anguish, but also made you who you are."

"I don't even know if I'm that self-reflective," Wyatt spoke up. "What if I don't know mine?"

"That will be of no consequence. The way this works is that I will merge your minds. One by one I will find your truth for you, in your memories, and will expose it to your fellow warriors. It will bring you trust, and it will shed any weight you are carrying. If you are to defeat my brother, this is our only course of action."

"No." Lucy croaked out. "I won't do it. Take all the blood you want, but my secrets are my own. I have a right to them."

Wyatt, Liv, and Theo all looked at her, concerned. Eli thought back to her confession in the storage closet about what happened to her friend, Jeremy. He understood her hesitation. He was scared as well, not looking forward to reliving his worst moment. He assumed it would be the night his parents died. Who would want to live through that twice?

Eli moved towards her. At that moment, all he wanted to do was hug her. To make her understand, she had nothing to hide. Instead, he stopped himself. This was not his burden to bear. All he could do was be there to help her lift it.

"Lucia, I truly am sorry," Athena spoke kindlier than she had since they'd been there. "To save the world, you must do this. There are no other options."

Lucy's eyes welled up, but she did nod at the goddess, accepting her fate. Athena guided the Five into a circle, all facing inwards at each other. She instructed them to hold hands with the person next to them.

"Alright," Athena said, "Let's begin."

Chapter Nineteen

"Why do I have to be first?" Theo looked around, panicked.

Eli and the others stood in the quad of a high school that he had never seen before. He looked up to find the others still standing in a circle with him. They dropped each other's hands and looked at Theo, waiting for him to continue.

"This is where I went to high school." He sighed. "And I'm willing to bet it's my sophomore year."
"How can you tell?" Lucy asked.
"That was when my mom died. And if the ritual calls for pain, this day is the perfect opportunity."

Theo led them inside the school. After walking down a long hallway, he finally stopped them, pointing to a young boy. The student placed his books in a locker and walked over to a set of double doors.

"That's little me." He told them.
"You're so cute!" Liv grinned at him. "Not that you aren't now, I mean."
"I get it," he assured her, giving her a small smile.

They followed the boy through the doors and found themselves in a gymnasium. There were fifteen kids, all shooting basketballs. Little Theo kept moving, heading straight into a locker room.

"I don't wanna go in there." Big Theo whispered.

"I think you have to, if that's what we're all here to see." Eli frowned. "We're with you though. You're safe."

Big Theo exhaled and nodded, resuming leading the group in the direction his counterpart had gone.

The locker rooms were darkened, the smell of men's body spray and sweat mingling in the air. Little Theo stood frozen in between a row of short lockers. Eli furrowed his brows, wondering what had stopped him. In the silence, he heard soft laughter coming from the showers.

"Nate?" Little Theo called softly.

There was a clamor as the water turned off, and around the corner appeared a taller boy, wearing only a towel wrapped around his waist.

"Oh. Hey, babe." The smile on Nate's face made it seem like he hadn't a care in the world, but the wet footsteps they heard running away from the scene said otherwise. "You're cutting it a little close today, huh? The bell rang five minutes ago."

"Well, I'm terribly sorry that I ran late and caught you in the shower with someone else. My bad, really." Sarcasm dripped from Little Theo's voice.

"What? You're acting crazy. I wasn't in the shower with anyone else." Nate shook his head, "Someone else was in a separate shower. They must've been running late too. I wouldn't do that to you."

"No, don't do that. I'm not stupid and I know this isn't

the first time either.”

“I don't think you're stupid, stop putting words in my mouth.” Nate threw his hands up. “All I said was you're crazy to be accusing me like that. It's always something with you.”

“Always something?” Little Theo took a step closer. “What the fuck is that supposed to mean.”

“You know what it means. You're always whining about something; you've been like this for weeks. Now you're trying to make me look like the bad guy.”

“Excuse me?”

“I know, I know, your mom died. I'm sorry about it, really, but it's been a month. Can't you just get over it already?”

Silence fell. Eli didn't need to see Little Theo's face to know what his reaction was.

Eli took a step forward, but then stopped in his tracks as he heard Athena's voice in his head.

“They can't see you, Eli. Even if they could, you can't help this. It has already happened to Theo before. It would not erase his pain.”

Eli shook his head and relaxed his fists, not even realizing that he had clenched them.

“I thought you loved me.” Little Theo said.

“I'm so sick of this.” Nate turned to leave. “You know what? Even if I *was* with someone else, can you blame me? Better than being sad all the time with you.”

“Don't ever speak to me again.”

“Oh fine, but don't come crawling back to me when nobody else wants to put up with you either.”

Nate finally left. Little Theo plopped down on the bench, placing his head in his hands and sobbing.

"Nate and I had been dating for six months when this happened." Big Theo's voice was hoarse. "For the record, he and Chaz Shaefer were dating the very next day, so I wasn't crazy."

"We didn't think you were." Liv wrapped an arm around him.

"He was there for me when my mom passed, at first, and I loved him. I thought he loved me, too. He was also my only friend, so the next two years were absolute hell. College was better, but even then, I wasn't really close with anyone else. At a certain point, I just adapted to survive."

Eli reached his hand out to His Theo, placing it on his shoulder. The others took a step closer to him as well as if they all just wanted him to feel their presence. So that he would know that he had their support. Theo looked at them, his eyes glistening.

"Thank you for being here."

The room swirled around them.

■■

"I can't do this." Liv's eyes filled with fear.

The Five had arrived at a small park near a pavilion. There appeared to be a family there, celebrating something. Because of the balloons and streamers, Eli guessed it was a birthday party.

Wyatt pulled Liv into a hug and kissed her forehead.

"It's going to be okay. We're all going to be here for you, no matter what." He promised.

Liv took a deep breath, exhaling slowly.

"This was my little sister Jesse's seventh birthday party that our dad threw for her," she began. "I was fifteen. That's us over there, with our dad."

Eli looked to where she was pointing and recognized Teenager Liv immediately. She was sitting at a picnic table, laughing with a small girl who looked almost exactly like her. Suddenly, a car came screeching into the parking lot, nearly knocking over a garbage post.

"Olivia Warren!"

A woman got out of the car and slung her purse over her shoulder, stumbling over to Teenager Liv and Jesse. Eli could tell from where he stood that the woman was completely drunk.

Teenager Liv looked up; panic was written on her face. "Mom?"

A tall man stood up and marched over to the woman, getting in between her and the girls.

"Judy, this is unacceptable." Liv's father said firmly. "The courts said—"
"I don't care a damn bit about what the courts said, Patrick. I'm here to talk to her."
"She's not speaking with you. Neither of them will ever again. You need help, Judy."

Teenager Liv guided Jesse over to her friends to play. Jesse hesitated, but after a nudge, she finally went. Teenager

Liv walked closer to her parents. Her dad saw her come to them and stood in front of her, protectively.

"Well, there she is. Loose Liv." Judy's face was red, and her words were full of malice. "Roger left me, and I know it was your fault, you stupid slut."

"Mom, listen, I don't know what happened with you and Roger—"

"Don't you dare say his name to me. You thought you were so cute and innocent when you testified against us, making up all kinds of lies. You were in love with him, admit it."

"Judy, I will not tell you again," Patrick said calmly. "You nced to leave now. I will call the police."

"'You have no right!"

"No." He responded, much less calm. "You have no right. After what you put our girls through. After you stayed with that disgusting man, you should have gone to jail. Now you show up here, drunk again, and want to throw around accusations at our seven-year-olds birthday party."

"No!" Judy pushed Patrick out of the way, headed for Liv. "She knows what she did!"

Teenager Liv's eyes went wide, just as Judy lunged at her.

Eli was so engrossed in what he was watching he didn't realize that the scream he heard was coming from Older Liv. He turned to see Wyatt hide her sobbing face in his chest, holding her. As he turned back, he understood. When Judy pushed Patrick, he had fallen on the edge of the pavilion's concrete floor. Judy stood in shock.

"It was an accident," she stammered. "I didn't mean to—"

"No, you meant it to be me. I got it." Teenager Liv

shouted at her in a rage, kneeling to check on Patrick. "Call 9-1-1!"

"If I call them, they'll arrest me!"

"Are you serious? He's going to die!"

With tears in her eyes, Teenager Liv pulled out her cellphone. Blood covered her hands from where she had held her dad's head.

Older Liv caught her breath long enough to speak.

"By the time the ambulance got here, it was already too late." She sobbed. "Mom went to prison for manslaughter, and Jesse and I went to live with dad's sister, our aunt. Mom still doesn't believe me to this day, but I never did anything with Roger. He was a drunk just like mom was, and he was a creep. I told the courts the truth because I was terrified of them both."

"I'm so sorry Liv." Lucy grabbed her arm and leaned into her.

"Thank you," Liv replied, before directing her next words to the sky, pleadingly. "Athena? Can we go now? I don't want to relive Jesse seeing this, please."

■ ■

"Wyatt Andrews!"

The Five stood on a city street, in front of a salon. An older woman was shouting Wyatt's name at the entrance.

"That's Annie. She was my mom's best friend, and she used to watch me when I was younger." Wyatt smiled and then pointed to a small child waddling up to the woman. "And that's baby me. I was three years old here."

Liv and Lucy gushed over how adorable he was. Wyatt shushed them and redirected their attention back to the memory.

"Boy, if you don't get your behind in here," the woman smiled and spoke with a similar twang to Wyatt's.

Baby Wyatt laughed and ran inside. The Five followed him in. The child hopped up into a barber's chair, grabbing a coloring book and crayons.

After seeing Theo and Liv's memories, Eli was on guard, waiting for the tragedy to strike. Wyatt must have sensed Eli's movements and placed a hand on his shoulder.

"Don't worry," he assured him. "This, luckily, was my only real trauma, and it was nothing compared to theirs."

Eli frowned at him. "You can't compare trauma. A scraped knee can hurt just as much as a headache, depending on who it's happening to."

"I appreciate that, but let's just watch."

The phone rang from across the salon. The older woman from before walked over and answered it. Eli heard her gasp, and she dropped the phone.

"Diana," she addressed one of the other stylists, "I need you to watch the salon for me and have Stacy cancel all of my appointments."

"Is everything okay?" The woman she had called Diana asked.

"No," Annie shook her head sadly. She walked over to Baby Wyatt and leaned down to reach his eye level. "Let's go get some ice cream, huh?"

Baby Wyatt gasped. His eyes lit up, and he grinned from ear to ear. The group followed Annie and the child to an ice cream shop a block away.

As Baby Wyatt shoveled chocolate ice cream into his mouth, Annie revealed the reason the Five were there.

"Baby boy, I'm gonna tell you something, but I need you to know that it's gonna be okay. Can you do that for me, pumpkin?"

Baby Wyatt nodded dramatically.

"I just got a call, and it was bad news." Annie reached out and grabbed his hand. "Your Grammy had an accident earlier."
"An askadent?"
"Yes, it's when something happens that wasn't supposed to."
"Like when we go to the store the udder day an forgot the milk?" Baby Wyatt tilted his head.
"Yeah, like that," Annie reached over and pushed his hair back. She took a deep breath and continued. "Your Grammy fell down, sweetheart, something pretty bad."

Baby Wyatt's eyes widened as he put another spoonful of ice cream in his mouth.

"The doctor's worked really hard to fix her," Annie's eyes welled up, "But she was a little too broken."
"Can I go see Gammy? I can try ta help." Eli heard Liv and Lucy sniffling beside him.
"No, baby. I'm so sorry but, Grammy's gone."
"I want Gammy." Baby Wyatt cried and threw his spoon down. "Take me to Gammy."

Annie let loose and cried with him. She whispered apologies to him and hugged him tightly.

"That was it for me," Adult Wyatt wiped a tear from his eye. "Like I said, not nearly as bad."

Eli stepped over to him and pulled him into a hug. Wyatt returned it, squeezing tightly.

■■

"Oh, no. No, no, no." Lucy turned to Eli, tears already in her eyes.
"What is it?"
"I'm so sorry." She whispered. "I didn't—"

Eli narrowed his eyes in confusion.

"Where are we?" Liv asked.

The Five could see nothing around them, only bright white space that seemed to go on for miles.

"This is the In-Between, isn't it?" Wyatt interrogated Lucy. "Apollo told me about this place. He said it was where gods come to hide or to think."
"Why would Lucy be here, then?" Theo asked, bewildered.
"There's my girl." A man's loud voice boomed from across the expanse.

Looking closer, they could see a Second Lucy standing with him. The Five walked closer.

"Is that—?" Liv's eyes widened.

"It is," Wyatt scowled. "That's Zeus."

Eli felt like he was going to throw up. He turned to Their Lucy, silently begging her to tell him that this wasn't what it looked like. That she wasn't working with the very monster that they needed to defeat. That she wouldn't betray them, or him, like that. Their Lucy's mouth was open, stammering, but she did not speak.

"Who are you? How did I get here?" Second Lucy glared.

"My name is Zeus. You are here because you have something I want," he stated, "and I believe I have something to offer you in return."

"Zeus." Second Lucy gasped. "What do you want from me?"

"I know that you recently met with Hermes and the others. I know that you also finally found the descendant of Demeter as well. You and the others will be embarking on your journey in two days, and I will need you to tell me where The Five are at all times."

"Yeah, right. I'm not going to betray everyone, Zeus. Nice try though, really." She turned to walk away.

"This is where I repeat, I believe I have something you want." Zeus stepped back and snapped his fingers.

As if opening a window, a square shape pulled apart through the white. Through it, there was a boy around their age, in chains. He looked like he was in a dungeon of sorts.

"Damien!" Second Lucy cried. She turned to Zeus, fury on her face. "You let him go or I swear—"

"Oh, sweetie," Zeus pouted at her. "You couldn't hurt me if you tried. If you want him to make it out of this alive, you'll do as I say. Otherwise..." He trailed off, and through the window, the boy began screaming in pain.

"Okay!" She shouted, tears in her eyes. "Okay, I'll do it."

"Fantastic. I knew you would make the right choice." Zeus closed the window. "Here's what will happen. Each night of your journey, I will pull you here from your sleep. You will report to me everything that you know. Where you are, where you're planning to go, and any information that may be of value to me. Then, when you wake up, you will remember nothing of this."

"Wait, what? You're going to erase my memory?"

"Dear, I can't have you spilling all of my secrets in a moment of weakness. You will only remember once you are back in this room."

Second Lucy wiped the tears from her cheeks, her breathing heavy. "Fine."

As Second Lucy gave Zeus all the information she had, the others encircled Their Lucy, their faces painted with shock and betrayal. Eli felt anger building up inside of him, burning at his throat and threatening to spill out from his eyes.

"Damien is my brother." Lucy squeaked out. "We got separated in the foster system after our parents deserted us and I thought I would never see him again. Zeus promised his safety."

"He's going to kill everyone on Earth!" Wyatt shouted. "You think he's gonna save a random boy who means nothing to him?"

"Please, you have to understand. He's the only family I have left."

"It's clear you know nothing about family, Lucy." Theo snapped.

"Hey!" Liv spoke up, in her defense, "You heard the same thing we did. Zeus wiped her memory every time she left."

"That doesn't matter." Wyatt glowered. "When she was here, she remembered. That means that she willingly betrayed us. Repeatedly."

"That's how all the monsters kept finding us." Eli realized. "They only appeared after you had slept. Does he know where we are now?"

Lucy looked down, nodding her head. The others looked at each other in panic.

"We'll deal with this later. Athena!" Theo called, "Bring us back!"

Chapter Twenty

"We have to get this weapon forged now." Eli insisted once they were all back in the cavern. "Will it work if we haven't seen my memory yet?"

"My dear boy, I am so sorry." Athena's face was grave. "Yours was not a memory. You are experiencing it right now and, I regret to tell you, it has only just begun."

Eli felt like he had been sucker-punched. After every disappointment in his life, his parent's death. Knowing for certain that Lucy's betrayal was his worst moment was too much for him to bear. The anger rose again, clawing its way through his heart. He shook his head furiously, attempting to knock loose every bad thought that was overloading his brain.

Now is not the time for this. We have to focus. Eli took a few deep breaths and cleared his throat, finally able to speak once more.

"Okay, let's do this then."
"Very well." Athena's face showed hints of worry as well. "Give me your hands."
"We need those to fight," Liv piped up.

"And I'm a goddess who can heal them. Now, we mustn't dawdle."

One by one, she sliced through their palms, spilling the blood in the same spot on the ground. Once the last of the blood had spilled, a blinding red light glowed from the puddle. It was so bright that the Five had to look away. Once they returned their attention to it, they saw a small hunting knife.

"That tiny thing is going to kill a god?" Theo raised his brows, picking the weapon up carefully and examining it.
"Kill him?" Athena replied. "Were you all expecting to kill Zeus this whole time?"
"Uh, yes? I thought that was the whole point." Eli answered.

Athena placed two fingers at her temple and rubbed, sighing. "I will never understand the hubris of mortals. You cannot kill a god, fools. The prophecy states you must defeat him. 'The Mighty will fall by the hands of the Five'. This knife won't kill him, but one stab will incapacitate him so that we may throw him into Tartarus."
"Oh, well, Lucy should do it then." Wyatt sneered. "She's used to stabbing people in the back."

Frustration and defeat were etched on Lucy's face. Without a word, she fled back up the stairs. Athena turned to the group and spoke sternly.

"That girl, your friend, was in an impossible situation. Let's not pretend that we would do anything less if the people we loved, more than anything, were in danger. In the meantime, she has helped each of you, saved each of you, and loved each of you. You are all within your rights to feel betrayed, hurt, angry, even. I truly hope each of you works through that with her. But she does not deserve the malice that is dripping from your tongues, nor the hatred that is being shown in your eyes."

Wyatt looked away, ashamed, his face turning a slight pink color. Eli was still as nauseous as he had been during the revelation. He felt betrayed, and it stung. What was worse, is that he also agreed with Athena. How on earth could he love and hate someone at the same time? Eli had never felt like this before, and it frustrated him. He felt angry, and then immediately felt guilty for feeling angry.

Various memories flooded his mind. Memories of their trip to Amsterdam, Lucy arguing with Wyatt about waffles, the night that she had spent in his bed, the guilt he had felt in her honor over Callie. Eli even remembered the look on her face the very first time they met. The mixture of beauty and mockery that always suited her so well. That couldn't possibly be the same girl that would do something like this to him. But the broken look on her face when she saw her brother made Eli's heart ache for her.

He shook his head, clearing his mind, and reminding himself to focus on the task at hand.

"We need to go. If Zeus knows where we are, he may already be on his way." Eli turned to address Athena directly.
"Will you help us fight?"
"Sadly, I cannot. I have done all that I am able, as have your ancestors. It is up to each of you from here on."
"Thank you very much for your help." Eli bowed to her.

Athena gave him a small, amused smile and tilted her head in a nod. Eli grabbed the knife from Theo, and the group headed up the stairs as well.

Chapter Twenty-One

Lucy's scream echoed through the cave just as the group reached the top of the steps. They took off at a run towards the opening, jumping over the stalagmites and drawing their weapons as they ran. The bats shrieked, diving at the group as they ran and only stopping when they finally reached sunlight.

Once outside, they skidded to a halt. Nearly fifty hoplites, just like the ones who fought Apollo, surrounded them.

In the middle of the warriors stood another tall man, his arm around Lucy, and a sword to her throat. The man wore a golden helmet with a red plume sticking out from the top. His face was arrogant, shoulders back as if he was posturing like a peacock.

"Drop your weapons, children." He bellowed.

The four warriors complied, thrusting their weapons to the ground.

"I'm so sick of asking this, but who is that?" Eli looked at Wyatt.
"I honestly have no clue," he responded.

"Foolish mortals. I am Ares, God of War!"

"Oh," Wyatt laughed, "That makes more sense. With the soldiers and all, I mean."

"I see my reputation as a strategist and leader of armies has preceded me." Ares held his head high.

"More like your reputation of being the weakest of all the Olympians." Wyatt pouted at him.

Eli's head snapped towards Wyatt in panic.

"What are you doing?" He hissed.

"I mean, come on. That's why you need so many soldiers to fight for you, right?" Wyatt continued. His voice filled with amusement as he spoke.

"Blasphemy!" The god threw Lucy towards the ground and stepped forward. "You dare to call me weak? I will gut you like a fish, boy!"

Wyatt smirked at him once Lucy was safely on the ground and swiftly kneeled to grab his bow.

"Apollo was right. It is easy to piss you off." He drew back his bow and fired an arrow directly at him, hitting him in the eye, then shouted over his shoulder at the others, "Get Lucy!"

Liv and Eli grabbed their swords and ran forward. Theo shape shifted into a giant lion, and charged forward at the hoplites, distracting them while Eli helped Lucy up.

"A Nemean Lion!" one soldier shouted. "That's impossible!"

Within moments, Lion Theo had taken out at least twenty of the hoplites, leaving carnage in his path. Many of the soldiers tried to stab him, but they left no marks on the golden fur. Once Lucy was on her feet, Liv and Eli went to help Lion Theo take on the rest of them.

Lucy went to help Wyatt with Ares, who had finally retrieved the arrow from his eye and was heading towards the boy menacingly. Just as Ares raised his sword to strike Wyatt down, Lucy tackled the god with all of her strength, knocking him to the ground, unconscious. Wyatt helped Lucy to her feet and nodded his appreciation. Lucy simply shrugged, and they both ran to help the others.

By the time they got there, only one soldier remained, who had fallen to his knees in surrender. Lion Theo walked towards him slowly, roaring fiercely in the hoplite's face. He shifted back into his human form and laughed.

"Well, go on." Theo motioned to the man. "Run away now."

The hoplite obeyed, darting back into the jungle.

"Stupid children," Ares grunted, rising from where he had fallen. "You can't stop us."

The god waved his hands, and the Five fell to their knees, screaming in pain.

"You dare to call me weak when I can do this to you? You are ants to me. Nothing more than pests to be exterminated. And my brother will see that you are."

Ares strode over and plucked the knife they had forged from Eli's pocket. He then yanked Lucy up by a fistful of her hair.

"In the meantime, he'll be pleased if I bring him home a treat, don't you think?"

"No!" Eli cried out as Ares and Lucy vanished, taking the weapon with them.

■■■

"What do we do?"

"I don't—I don't know," Wyatt's voice trailed off.

"What do we do?!" Eli asked again, enunciating each word, and pacing back and forth.

"I said I don't know!" Wyatt shouted back at him. "The prophecy said it all ends here, on this stupid island. This wasn't supposed to happen!"

"We just go get her, right?" Liv offered, her voice dripping with worry. "We just go to wherever they took her and fight Zeus there."

"How are we gonna get there, Liv? Lucy was the one who did the portals!"

"Okay, first off," Liv glared her eyes at Wyatt, "don't speak to me that way. I'm just trying to help."

Wyatt recoiled. "You're right, I'm sorry. Everyone, just give me a minute. Let me think."

"Ares most likely took Lucy to Mount Olympus, right? That's where Zeus lives?" Eli fidgeted impatiently.

"Eli, please." Wyatt shushed him. "I promise I'll figure this out. Just give me one more minute."

Eli took a seat on the ground and put his head in his hands. He tried to control his breathing and slow down his heartbeat, but it was no use. No matter how angry he was, the thought of actually losing Lucy was a million times worse. It took everything in him not to cry out of frustration.

"I've got it," Wyatt finally spoke again. "Ares probably took Lucy to Mount Olympus.

"You don't say." Eli sarcastically interrupted.

"Just listen. Mount Olympus is in Greece. We just have to go back the same way and then go north."

"That's four days," Eli exclaimed. "She could be dead by then. Hell, the entire world could be."

"Eli's right," Theo said. "We need a faster way to get there."

Wyatt put his hand to his head. "Theo! That's it!"

"What?"

"You turned into a Nemean Lion," Wyatt said. "That's a mythical creature. So, you can turn into other mythical creatures too, theoretically. Possibly even one's that could fly."

"Huh, I guess I could." Theo looked surprised at himself.

He walked a few steps away from them and closed his eyes, but nothing happened.

"Damnit."

"What were you aiming for? Maybe that's the issue." Eli asked.

"A dragon," Theo said sheepishly. Eli, Wyatt, and Liv couldn't help themselves but laugh.

"Yeah," Wyatt sighed, "maybe we try something a little smaller. Can you do a Pegasus? That would carry all of us, I think."

Theo closed his eyes again and shifted. Standing in front of them now was the largest white horse Eli had ever seen, its wings beautiful, spanning at least twenty feet on each side.

"Alright, let's go." Wyatt motioned to the others.

As he and Liv climbed on, they realized that the weight was taking a toll on Pegasus Theo.

"We're gonna have to leave everything except our weapons," Wyatt stated.

"That's not the only issue," Eli followed up, "I definitely weigh more than your bags do. I don't think he can take all three of us."

Wyatt thought for a moment, a sly smile appearing on his face. "You mean, he can't take all three of us *humans*."

"You've gotta be kidding me."

"Come on, Chicken Little. Do what you do best."

"Humiliating," Eli grumbled. "Just plain humiliating."

Chapter Twenty-Two

The clouds flew by like an ocean of white foam as Liv and Wyatt rode on Pegasus Theo, with Chicken Eli tucked securely in Liv's lap. The blue waves rippled miles beneath them, though Eli could not allow himself to look down at them.

The journey that had taken them days turned into a three-hour flight, and as they got closer to their destination, Eli let out a squawk unintentionally at the sight. Mount Olympus was more wondrous than he could have ever imagined. The higher they flew up the mountain, the more adrenaline shot through him. He worried for a moment that his tiny chicken heart was going to give out on him.

Finally, the foursome made it to the top, and Pegasus Theo landed them on the clouds right in front of a large pair of golden gates. He and Chicken Eli both changed back into their human forms.

"Okay, we need to make a plan." Wyatt pulled them into a huddle.

"Easy," Eli began. "We get past the gates, find Lucy, and steal back the weapon. Then we use the weapon to take out Zeus, and we're all back in the penthouse by dinnertime."

"I admire your process," Wyatt smirked, "But we need to plan how we're going to do all of that."

"I can handle step one," Liv said. "Alexiares and Anicetus guard the gates. I can use the belt to get us past them."

Wyatt looked uncomfortable for a moment, but he agreed.

"Okay, so that's one down. I think we should split up for steps two and three. Eli, Liv, go find Lucy. Theo and I will find the weapon."

"Sounds good." Theo nodded. "Then we can take care of step four together."

"The question now is, where do we go once inside?" Theo queried.

"The gatekeepers typically know all the goings-on for the inside. Liv, can you try to get it out of them?"

"I won't have to try," she said confidently.

"Good point." Wyatt did genuinely smile at that. "Okay, so let's go."

"Should we do a cheer?" Liv asked, earning skeptical looks from the boys. "Since we're in a huddle, I mean. We put all of our hands in the middle and shout, 'Go Five!' or 'Go Team!' or something."

"I think we're okay." Eli smiled warmly at her. "Maybe next time."

"Fine," she sighed. "Don't look at me and let's get this show on the road."

While Liv distracted the guards, Theo, Eli, and Wyatt snuck past them. Wyatt waved to Liv once they were safely inside. She blew a kiss at the guards and hurried to join her friends, taking off her belt as she went.

"Lucy's being kept with Damien in the dungeon. The stairs down to it are to the left at the end of the hall. The dagger is with Ares, who is meeting Zeus in the garden. If you go down the main hallway, it'll be on your right."

Wyatt grabbed Liv and pulled her into a long kiss. Eli and Theo looked away awkwardly.

"Be careful," he urged.
"Always," she promised as she pulled away.

The four all nodded to each other and split off. Liv and Eli went left, sticking close to the walls, moving as silently as possible. Anytime they heard a voice, they stopped and ducked behind one of the many plants lining the hall. Finally, they made it to a large wooden door at the end of the path. Eli pushed it open and saw the stone staircase. He and Liv carefully descended it.

A wide metal door stood at the foot of the steps. Eli yanked at the handle, but the door wouldn't budge.

"Augh, it's locked." Eli sighed in frustration.
"Yeah, well, it's a jail cell." The sarcastic voice that Eli had grown to love echoed from inside the cell.
"Lucy!" Liv exclaimed in a hushed tone. "Thank gods you're okay. We're here to rescue you."
"Really?" Her voice seemed so genuinely surprised that it made Eli's chest hurt.
"Yeah, of course," Liv replied, reaching into her pocket. She pulled out a bobby pin and kneeled at the lock. "Give me a second. I think I can get this."
"Okay, there's no way that a prison built by the gods is gonna be that easy to—"
"Got it!" Liv bragged as Eli heard a loud click.
"Well, I've been wrong before." He pulled the door open and stepped inside.

Lucy was sitting on a small cot, her leg chained to the wall. Eli sucked in a breath at the sight of her face. Her eyes were dark, and she had bruises all over her. There was a cut at the edge of her mouth and one above her brow as well.

"Who did that to you?" He asked quietly, feeling his hands clench at his sides.

"A few of the hoplites," she answered weakly. "Ares wanted me punished before locking me up. He said that Zeus felt betrayed that you all found out he had been using me."

"Oh, he feels betrayed?" Eli spat the words out. He saw Lucy cringe and he cleared his throat. "I'm sorry. Let's just get you out of here."

He raised his sword and cut through the chain holding her captive. Liv helped her to her feet while Eli placed his hands, healing her wounds. Once she could stand on her own, they left.

"Wait," Lucy stopped them just before the exit, nodding towards a corner of the cell. "We have to save Damien."

It was only then that Eli noticed the boy curled up in the corner, asleep and shivering. Damien looked so much worse than when they had seen him in Lucy's truth vision, his eyes sunken in and his clothes soaked in blood. Eli imagined how confused he must be. How terrified.

"There's a door at the top of the stairs." Eli nodded. "You can portal him out from there, but we have to do this quickly."

Lucy exhaled, looking at Eli with gratitude. "Okay, let's go."

Eli helped Lucy lift her brother and carry him up the stone steps. Once at the top, Lucy worked her magic, and moments later, she deposited her brother safely into a hospital room.

"I'll come back for you, I promise," Lucy whispered as she retreated into the dungeon.

Liv, Eli, and Lucy crept back up the stairs and back down the hallway they had come from. When the trio arrived at the doors to the garden, they found Wyatt waiting outside. Wyatt ran and hugged Liv, kissing her forehead. When they pulled away, Wyatt surprised them all by pulling Lucy into a hug as well.

"I'm glad you're okay, Red." He said as he pulled away.
"Uh, thank you,' Lucy said, startled by the interaction. "Same here."
"Did you get the knife? Where's Theo?" Eli bombarded him with questions.
"Would you keep it down?" Wyatt whispered. "Theo should be out any minute. When we peeked in, Ares and Zeus were in there. The knife was on a table farther away. The only way we could come up with to get it was to have Theo change. He's in there as a squirrel right now. He should have been out a few minutes ago, but I've got five more minutes before he said I could go in after him."
"Okay, how is he getting back out, though?" Lucy asked.
"What do you mean?" Wyatt narrowed his eyes.
"He's a squirrel. And the door is closed."
"Ah, crap."

Wyatt slowly creaked the door open, and Squirrel Theo darted out towards them, dragging the knife behind him. He switched back and glared at Wyatt.

"I've been waiting, terrified, for ten minutes."

"I'm sorry," Wyatt stammered, "I didn't think that part through. But you got it and you're safe. That's what matters, right?"

"Sure," Theo threw his hands up, "whatever you say. But Ares left while I was in there, and he said something—"

"You can tell us when we get back to safety." Wyatt interrupted. "Luckily, I don't think anyone even knows we were here."

"I'm guessing someone does." A loud voice boomed from behind them.

Chapter Twenty-Three

The Five turned and took a step back against the garden door, raising their weapons. Zeus stood in front of them, his face stoic, eyes piercing.

"Well, it is nice to meet you all, finally. Except for Lucia, of course. We're old friends."

Zeus was larger than Eli recalled from Lucy's memory. He towered over them, his muscles making up about fifty percent of his torso. Eli felt Lucy and Theo making small, slow movements behind the group and willed himself not to turn around or draw attention.

"Sorry, we can't say the same." Liv glowered at the god.

Eli admired her bravery. It was all he could do not to throw up on the spot.

"Oh, come now, Olivia. Aren't you at least a little excited to meet me?" Zeus smirked at her, taking a step closer.
"You wish," she retorted.

"Well then, it seems I will have to work harder to impress you."

With a snap of the god's fingers, Wyatt's arm cracked, and he screamed out in pain, grabbing at it with his other hand. Liv rushed to his side to comfort him. Eli reached out and grabbed his hand, his eyes staying glued to Zeus. Wyatt squeezed his eyes shut, and moments later, he let go of Eli's hand and stood up straight once more.

"We're not scared of you," Wyatt's voice cracked, but he stood firm, raising his bow.
"You will be." Zeus raised his fingers again, but the arrow interrupted him just before he could snap them.

The shot hit him square in the face. Lucy rushed past Eli, hurling herself toward the god. Zeus grunted and reached for the arrow, yanking it out and throwing it on the ground.

"I'm going to rip you each apart limb by limb." He barked.

Lucy cried out as she leaped up and drove the knife into Zeus's chest. The god's eyes rolled back, and he slumped to the ground. She stepped back towards the others, all of them standing in shocked silence.

"Is-is that it?" Eli asked, practically holding his breath.

"No," Theo responded, earning him confused looks from the rest of the group.

Zeus grunted from where he kneeled. His arms and head hung limply. Eli almost wanted to walk over and poke him to make sure he really couldn't get back up.

"What do you mean?" Lucy exclaimed. "I stabbed him, we won. That was the entire mission."

"That's what I was trying to tell you guys," Theo's voice broke. "Ares had said something when I was in there. There was someone else on their side, someone who had helped Zeus with the plan. Zeus was never the only one we needed to defeat."

"What?" Eli asked. "Who else did we need to stop?"

Just then, large doors at the end of the hallway swung open. A figure shrouded in a black hood stepped out from the shadows of the doorway, sauntering towards them. Beneath the hood, a woman's voice emitted a wicked laugh.

"Well done, children." The voice said. Eli froze, his pulse racing at the recognition of the voice.

The figure reached its hands up and pulled off the hood, revealing the all too familiar face underneath.

Eli felt his heart leap to his throat.

"Demeter?"

• •

Demeter walked over to Zeus and retrieved the knife from his chest. She helped him to his feet and pulled out a handkerchief, wiping his blood off of the blade. With a flick of her wrist, the Five fell to their knees.

Eli groaned in pain at the force in which he hit the ground. His stomach was doing somersaults and he could feel tears stinging his eyes, threatening to spill over at any moment. Any kindness he had ever seen in Demeter was gone, leaving a cold, empty shell in its place.

"What—the actual fuck—is going on?" Lucy hissed through her teeth.

"Language, Lucia." Demeter's eyes darkened, and she waved her hand once more.

Eli heard Lucy grunt and looked over to see the girl could no longer open her mouth.

"That's better," the goddess continued. "Now, Zeus, we really should be going. What would you like to do with the children?"

"Can I not simply kill them, sister?" Zeus pouted at her.

"Death would be too easy," Demeter smirked. "And they did such a good job retrieving our weapon, did they not?"

Eli looked over at the others, their faces each racked with betrayal and confusion. Wyatt cleared his throat.

"I'm sorry, goddess, your weapon?" the boy asked carefully.

Demeter threw her head back and laughed. "Oh, look at them, Zeus, so stupid. It's almost endearing."

"Almost," Zeus grumbled.

"Yes, Wyatt, I will do you a service by explaining. Thank you for asking politely." Demeter continued, giving a pointed look at Lucy. "The prophecy to bring each of you together was, simply put, fake. It's quite funny, really. Ales is the name of a goat on my farm. Zeus and I planted the foresight ourselves decades ago."

"But you said—and Athena—all of this was fake?" Eli's thoughts moved faster than his mouth could voice them.

"Oh, Athena didn't know. Serves her right for always acting so high and mighty. Goddess of Wisdom, my ass." Zeus smirked, then continued. "Demeter and I needed the Five to forge this knife. Not to stop me, but to grant us the exact weapon that we needed."

"But if there's no prophecy, why would you need the five of us?" Eli asked.

"There was a prophecy." Demeter sneered. "Just not the one that each of you fools believed. Zeus, please."

Demeter waved her brother forward. Zeus took a step and postured, pulling out a small scroll. He opened it and read.

"Rivalry, hatred, pride, and deceit, this tale can only end in defeat.

In Thessaly, the Children of Myths will see a path does forge beneath their feet.

The Isle of Extinction is the journey's end, where friend is foe, and foe is friend.

A weapon is forged when the blood spills and secrets kept are truths revealed.

When the Five find the truth that tears them apart, the weapon arrives right back at the start.

Find the cracks hidden within the facade, or the Underworld falls at the hand of a god."

The Five gawked in silence as Zeus read. Eli breathed heavily, trying to make sense of the truth now before him.

"The Underworld?" Wyatt's voice croaked through the silence. "Destroying the Underworld is your grand plan?"

"It is the justice that Hades deserves," Demeter said angrily. "He took something from both of us, and now we will take everything from him."

"No," Liv interrupted, shaking her head, "You can't do that, though. All of those souls, where would they go?"

"Insufferable mortal. Trying to tell us, the gods of old, what we can and cannot do."

Demeter walked closer to the Five, leaning down towards Liv. She slapped the girl across the face, then grabbed her chin and looked directly into her eyes.

"Here's a fun thought for you Olivia; I don't give a damn about the souls. They can wander around the shores for eternity, for all I care. I will have my daughter back, and our treasonous siblings will be gone for good."

"How?" Wyatt attempted to draw her attention from Liv, who was now cowering in tears. "Gods can't be killed."

Demeter took a step back from the group. "I'm bored with this, Zeus. Let us go. We will strip the Five of their powers and leave them on the Plains of Thessaly where they started."

"Wait, please." Eli strained, wincing at how broken his voice sounded.

"Oh, my poor Eli."

For a moment, Eli saw a flicker of something familiar in Demeter's eyes. Before he could recognize what it was, it disappeared, and her eyes narrowed.

"You believed you were special. That you were chosen as part of an epic story. But this is nothing more than another Greek tragedy."

Demeter flicked her hand one last time, and Eli had no time to respond before everything went black.

Chapter Twenty-Four

Eli squinted his eyes as he awoke. He sat up and recognized the plains surrounding him. A chill swept through the air as the sun set behind the darkened skies. The first time he had been here was in the light of day. The sun had been high, and his hopes had been higher. Now it was all just a bittersweet memory.

Eli stood up, checking on the others. Wyatt and Theo lay a few feet away from him, still knocked out cold. Eli rose to his feet, trying to take a better look around, but he couldn't find Lucy or Liv.

"Hey, guys, get up." Eli walked over to Theo, kneeling to shake him awake.

"What—" Theo groggily sat up, and Eli heard Wyatt groan from where he lay.

A few moments later, all three boys were on their feet.

"I feel like I got hit by a truck." Wyatt rubbed his head. "Is everyone else alright?"

"As okay as I can be, but I can't see Lucy or Liv anywhere," Eli said sadly.

"What?" Wyatt's gaze darted around the plains. He shouted, "Liv? Liv, where are you?"

"We'll find her, Wyatt," Theo reassured him.

"Something tells me that if Demeter wanted them dead, she would have killed them in front of us to make a point. Let's just look around and check the monastery before we panic, okay?"

Wyatt took a deep breath and nodded. Eli could see his eyes watering and felt for the boy. He was concerned about Lucy, especially given her history with Zeus. The thought that she was gone again was too much to bear. Eli followed Wyatt's lead and inhaled deeply as well.

The boys split up to look, Eli heading to the monastery while the other two checked the plains surrounding them. Eli called out to Lucy and Liv as he walked, his shoulders heavy and his body exhausted.

Once Eli made it to the monastery, he knocked on a large wooden door at the front of the building. The doors swung open and out stepped a larger man in long black robes. A monk, Eli realized. The man asked something in Greek, and Eli silently cursed himself for not sending Wyatt this way instead.

"I'm sorry, I don't—" Eli stammered out.
"Ah, you speak English?" The man smiled. Eli let out a sigh of relief and nodded.
"I'm looking for my friends. We got split up, and I was hoping they would've come here."
The man raised his eyebrows. "That girl with the demon tongue is your friend?"
"Yes!" Eli exclaimed, sending a silent thank you to the heavens. "That's Lucy. Is she here?"
"Unfortunately, she is. Please, come in." The monk opened the door wider for Eli to enter.

Eli saw a large church right at the entrance with sun catchers and high ceilings. The sight was breathtaking. The monk led him down a long hallway, the man finally stopping them at the doorway into what looked like a small cafeteria. Sitting at one of the wooden tables were the girls, Liv's head resting on the tablecloth while Lucy stroked her friend's hair.

Eli stopped the monk from interrupting them, taking a moment to watch the exchange. He felt an ache in his chest at the sight of Lucy, wanting nothing more than to turn around and leave her. To keep her there, safe in the monastery, away from what was coming next. But leaving her there wouldn't solve anything, it would only make her angry. *Dead or furious? Which one is worse?* Finally, he nodded to the monk.

"Ladies," the monk spoke.

The girls looked up, and Eli gave a small wave. Lucy's eyes were tired, but even Eli could not mistake the gleam in them. She rose from the table and ran to him, throwing her arms around his neck.

"Thank heavens you're okay," Lucy whispered over his shoulder.

Eli hugged her back, inhaling deeply and not once caring about pretenses or his nerves. The honesty in their embrace overcame him, knowing at that moment that if he had one wish, it would be to keep holding her like this forever.

Once the two eventually parted, Lucy pulled him over to the table.

"We woke up here only a short bit ago," Lucy explained as they sat. "The monks were kind enough to bring us inside while we were unconscious. They made food too.

Where are the others?"

"They're out searching for you both in the plains. If you're feeling up to it, Liv, I think you should go out and check for them. It would help Wyatt a lot to see you right now."

"It would help me too, I think." Liv agreed and stood, leaving Eli and Lucy alone in the dining hall.

"I'm glad you're okay," Eli whispered. "I was terrified when we couldn't find you."

"Eli, I'm so sorry," Lucy said suddenly, tearing up. "For what I did, for helping Zeus. We never had time to...I just need you to know. If it weren't for Damien—"

"I know." He interrupted her, reaching out his hand to graze a stray tear from her cheek.

It reminded him of the red caterpillar he wiped away from her face on his training day. It had only been a few days before, but to Eli, it felt like it had been a lifetime.

"I understand why you did it, and why you couldn't tell us."

Lucy bit her lip, her eyes filled with worry. "Athena said that was your moment. Out of everything that has ever happened in your life, my hurting you was the worst. I hate myself, that I could be capable of that."

"You shouldn't hate yourself. I definitely don't."

"After that? How could you not?"

"There are many things I feel for you." Eli looked directly into her eyes. "For a bit there, yeah, hatred was one of them. That emotion lost out to a few stronger ones though."

Lucy gave a small smile, sniffling. "Oh yeah? Which emotions won?"

"Wouldn't you like to know?" Eli teased.

"I would," she whispered in reply, leaning in closer to

him.

"Careful, Lucy. What would the monks think?"

"They'd probably think that this is super awkward."

The pair jumped apart as they heard Wyatt's voice. They turned to see Wyatt, Theo, and Liv standing in the doorway, each of them smirking.

"Impeccable timing, as always." Theo chuckled.

Chapter Twenty-Five

"Okay, I know we're tired, but we need a plan." Wyatt took a sip of his water and reached for more bread.

The monks had made enough food to feed an army. Which, ironically, was what they would need to fight Demeter and Zeus, Eli thought to himself.

"I just can't believe Demeter was on his side the whole time. And the prophecy, I mean, come on. Can I reel from that before we move on?" Lucy placed her fork down beside her plate.

"You've got five seconds to reel." Wyatt allowed. "But then we need to focus. We can't let them destroy the Underworld or kill the other gods. We know that much. So, what *can* we do from here?"

"We need to contact one of our ancestors," Theo suggested. "Can we pray to them? Does that work?"

"It usually would," Wyatt replied, "but I've been praying to Apollo since we woke up here and got nothing. That either means it doesn't work without our powers or…"

"Or they could already be in trouble." Liv finished the thought. "I think our only option is to get back to the Underworld and find one of them. They can give us our powers back, and we can use the knife on Demeter this time."

"If we can even find one that we can trust," Eli said sadly.

"Hey," Wyatt looked at him sympathetically, "I'm sorry about Demeter, but you still have a lot of people you can trust. Don't let her take that away from you, too."

Eli pursed his lips, looking away.

"I wonder why Zeus is even helping her." Theo mused through a mouthful of food. "According to Apollo, Zeus was always jealous of Hades, anyway."

"Mm," Lucy agreed with Wyatt, "That makes sense. Since his relationship with Hera was shit and Hades and Persephone actually loved each other. That, and the whole sibling rivalry thing."

"Where is Hera in all this again?" Liv asked.

"On the other side of the world, hopefully," Wyatt answered. "The last thing we need is her getting involved."

"Either way, we're the only ones who can stop both of them," Eli said. "And probably Ares and Hephaestus, too."

"But now we're going in circles." Lucy sighed. "Because we still have to figure out how we're supposed to get to the Underworld to stop them."

She fidgeted with her hands and Eli imagined it probably frustrated her she could no longer make portals. He reached out and placed his hand on hers.

"Gross." Liv teased, and Eli retracted his hand quickly. Lucy and Liv both dissolved into giggles.

"Guys, can we please stay on track?" Wyatt scowled at both of them. "This is 'end of the world' serious."

It was serious before, was what Eli wanted to say, but even he knew in his heart that it wasn't true. This was far grimmer. There was no prophecy on their side this time, no guiding hands telling them what they needed to know, or even where to go.

"How do we get to the Underworld?" Theo posed. "Short of dying, I mean."

Eli's eyes met Wyatt's. Wyatt glared at him in return and shook his head. Eli frowned and widened his eyes. Finally, Wyatt sighed.

"Yes, Eli. Theoretically, it would work. But you would still be dead."

"Wait, what's happening?" Lucy snapped her gaze towards Eli, her eyes narrowed.

"If that's the only way to do it…" Eli trailed off.

"We can't just kill ourselves," Liv interjected.

"I agree. Only one of us needs to go."

"Eli…"

"No, Theo, I'm serious. We have to get to Hades to warn him, and if we can defeat Demeter and Zeus, we can ask one of the other gods to bring me back. They've done it before, right?" Eli looked at Wyatt.

"In certain circumstances, yes." Wyatt's eyes looked tired. "But we have no way of knowing if they even can bring you back. It's too dangerous."

"But—"

"No," Lucy said with finality, stamping her foot on the ground like a child. "We will figure this out in any other way possible."

Eli felt a burning sensation rising to his throat, but he conceded, knowing he could never convince them.

"Fine. I promised the monks I'd help them gather firewood after dinner, anyway. You guys let me know what you figure out."

"Eli," Lucy called after him. He turned to face her,

biting at his lip.

"I'll be back soon."

The lie flowed from his lips with ease. *Another trait I must have received from Demeter.*

Eli left, exhaling a breath he didn't know he'd been holding in. The monks had never asked him for help. It was the only thing he could think of that would get him away from his friends.

He left the monastery, opening the front door as quietly as he could. The chilly winds whipped at Eli's face as he walked out onto the plains, not even sure where he was going. He picked a spot on a nearby hill to sit and watch the ocean.

"Is this seat taken?" Eli turned to see Wyatt standing behind him.

"Be my guest. Where'd you get that?" Eli nodded to the bottle in his hands.

Wyatt sat beside Eli and popped open the cork on top.

"I stole it from the monk's ritual stash. That may get me thrown into Tartarus, but it'll taste good in the meantime."

He offered the bottle over, and Eli grabbed it, taking a swig. The burning sensation in his chest returned, but at least this time, he knew what was to blame.

"So, what do you think the last part of the actual prophecy meant?" Eli asked. "It's been playing in my head since we heard it. I feel like it's supposed to help us somehow."

"Find the cracks hidden in the facade?" Wyatt clarified. "It could mean anything. Zeus' facade, Demeter's facade. It could mean that we were supposed to find the cracks in Demeter's facade and that now we're too late."

"But?" Eli prodded.

"But if you feel like it's important, then it probably is. It's okay to trust your gut."

Eli understood he wasn't just talking about the prophecy. When he had met Demeter, he had his guard up. He had allowed his want of a loving maternal figure to cloud his judgment, and now he was dealing with the guilt of that mistake. Eli hoped that the guilt would make it easier for him to do what he needed to do next.

"I know you're going to do it, anyway," Wyatt said softly after a moment.

"Is that why you're here? They sent you out to check on me?"

"Nah, they didn't catch on. They think I'm helping the monks, too."

Eli let out a sigh of relief.

"This will hurt them though when they inevitably find out." Wyatt took the bottle back. "Lucy, especially."

"I can handle her being upset with me." Eli decided. "As long as I'm taking a chance to make sure she doesn't die. To make sure none of you do."

The boys sat in silence for a few moments, passing the bottle back and forth.

"You didn't answer my question before about why you came out here."

Wyatt gritted his teeth as his eyes watched the stars.

"We both know this is the only move. And…"
"And?"
Wyatt's voice was quiet. "I just thought it would be better if you didn't die alone."

Eli felt his throat tighten, overcome with emotion. Looking at Wyatt, he no longer saw the arrogant bully of a man before him. Just a friend, someone he could depend on. Eli dared to say he was grateful that Wyatt had joined him.

"Plus," Wyatt nudged him, "I actually have the coins, so you won't die for no reason."

Eli laughed and nudged him back. He thanked his lucky stars that Wyatt was a know-it-all since he had completely forgotten about the coins until that moment. He stood and helped Wyatt up as well.

"So, how are we doing this?" Wyatt asked.
Eli unsheathed his sword and handed it to him. "Quickly, I hope."
Wyatt took the sword and held it at Eli's throat. "Be careful, and good luck. We'll be waiting for you here."

Eli nodded, squeezing his eyes, and bracing himself.

"Sweet dreams, Waldo."

Chapter Twenty-Six

Whatever Eli imagined death would be like, it did not come close to what it truly was. He stood on the shores, the sky a grayish-green color surrounding him. The air was humid, and the stench of rotting fish and saltwater was enough to make him gag.

When Eli had first woken, he choked, coughing up the Obol that Wyatt had stuffed in his mouth. He could still feel the pain in his throat where the blade had sliced, making it hard for him to swallow. More than the sensation around his throat, his entire body felt broken and disjointed, aching with every forward motion he took on the shore.

Up ahead, he saw the small boat. A large, cloaked man stood on the sand beside it, holding a lantern. The imagery reminded him of a tarot card he had seen when he was a child, at a psychic fair, with his mom. He didn't remember the name of the card but could hear the psychic's voice, clear as a bell, telling his mom to look for answers within herself.

Eli stepped closer to the man, asking timidly, "Excuse me, are you Charon?"

The man shoved the lantern toward Eli swiftly, and a pair of bright yellow eyes glared from underneath his cloak.

"Do you have the fare?"

Eli held out the obol, and Charon snatched it from his hand. He turned the coin over a few times, sniffed it, and then placed it in his pocket.

"Can I get on the boat now?"
"No."
Eli furrowed his brow. "But I died. And I paid you."
"You were not on the schedule. The boat moves with the schedule. You must wait here for the next scheduled death, and hope that person has their payment as well."
"I don't have time for that!" Eli panicked. "I have to see Hades as soon as possible."
"You *want* to see Hades?" Charon asked. "What did you say your name was?"
"I didn't, but it's Elias Riley."
Charon sighed. "You should have led with that."

The ferryman pulled the boat closer to them and helped Eli step aboard, muttering something about wasting his time. Charon grabbed an oar and sat on the bench next to Eli, placing the lantern at the front of the vessel.

"Please keep your arms and feet inside of the boat at all times. Your estimated time of arrival is whenever we get there."

Off they went. The farther down the river they got, the better Eli felt, his throat no longer raspy and his stomach no longer knotted. As they glided down the cascading water, Eli gaped at the bird's-eye view of the Underworld.

However marvelous he thought it before was nothing compared to seeing it from above. The entire Underworld was surrounded by the cosmos. A giant floating rock in the middle of a star-ridden sea. The rivers that flowed through the land dropped off the edges, falling endlessly into the abyss below.

As the boat pulled in front of Hades' home, it stopped. Charon nodded to Eli to disembark.

"Knock first," Charon advised once Eli was on solid ground. The boat spun around, heading back to the shores above.

Eli started up a long, winding pathway to the front door. As he walked, he felt something dripping on him from above.

"That's strange," he thought aloud, more droplets falling. "I didn't think it could rain in the Underworld."
"It can't." Eli heard the voice to his left.

He turned and saw a tall woman with brunette locks flowing down to her ankles. Eli recognized her immediately. She had the same green eyes as her mother.

"Persephone." He whispered.

The goddess wore a crown of flowers and sat on a stone bench, in what Eli believed was a garden, if not for the ground made of stone and the lack of nature.

"Hello, Eli." Her voice was like a song. "My mother has told me much about you."
"Your mother."

Eli's stomach dropped, wondering suddenly if this was a trap. It would make sense, he thought, with how easily Charon brought him here.

He calmed himself down and smiled politely, keeping his guard up.

"Yes," Persephone replied peacefully. "She was very excited to meet you and guide you to fulfill the prophecy. It was all she talked about the entire spring season." The goddess stood and walked toward Eli.

"You said it doesn't rain here." Eli did not want to talk about the prophecy nor Demeter for that matter. Not until Hades was there as well. "Was it water from the river that was dripping on me, then?"

"No." Her smile wavered. "When you enter the Underworld, every tear shed for you after your death will fall from the sky, like your own personal rain cloud. Someone who loves you is grieving their loss."

"That's so sad." Eli frowned, realizing the others must have noticed he was gone.

"It can be, but most mortals find comfort in it. They're said to have a sense of peace once the day finally comes that there is no more rain, because that is to mean that their loved ones are finally happy once more." She extended her hand towards the castle. "Shall we?"

Persephone led Eli up the stone steps to the front door, pausing once they reached it.

"Go ahead," she nudged. "Knock first."

Eli looked at her skeptically. "That's what Charon told me, too. Don't you live here, though?"

"I do, but that does not make me the owner of the home. It is polite to let the owner know someone is there to see them," The goddess smiled at him reassuringly, "and Hades is very much someone who likes good manners."

"Okay." Eli trailed off, reaching for the knocker, and banging it against the wooden door three times.

The door swung open so quickly that a gust of wind nearly knocked Eli from his feet. Persephone stepped inside first, beckoning Eli to follow.

Inside, Eli found himself in an enormous marble-floored foyer. He couldn't help but gawk, thinking that his entire house could fit in this one room at least ten times. There was a staircase in the middle of the room, with aisles leading off of each side, red carpet, and beautifully decorated banisters lining the walkways.

Almost as soon as the front door shut, they heard barking from down one of the many hallways. If Eli still had a life, it would have flashed before his eyes as he watched a three-headed dog, the size of a city bus, barreling towards them. Once the dog reached them, Persephone cooed and petted each one behind their ears.

"This is Cerberus." Persephone introduced. "He's harmless as long as you're not trying to escape death."

Eli chuckled and leaned his hand forward slowly, letting the middle dog head sniff him.

"Hello, my love." Hades' voice boomed from the top left of the staircase.

The god descended to the first floor, only noticing Eli after he greeted Persephone with a kiss.

"You must be Elias."
"Just Eli is fine, sir." He trembled as Hades got closer. "I'm sorry but, how did you guys know I would be here?"
"How did we know?" Hades raised an eyebrow.
"I only ask," Eli added hastily, "because I've been through something recently that I came to warn you about, actually. So, you already knowing I would be here is terrifying if I'm honest. I don't think I can die again, so I'm not worried about you killing me, but you could plan to take me to Tartarus and if that's the case then I have to warn you, I'm gonna complain and fight you the entire way there."

Hades and Persephone looked at each other, both tightening their lips into a thin line as if amused by Eli's ramblings.

"Poseidon was right. You talk a lot when you're nervous." Hades chuckled. He took a step closer to Eli, and leaned down slightly, looking him straight in the eyes. "I am not taking you to Tartarus. We knew you were coming because Thanatos, the god of Death, told us he sensed your presence on the beach. I told Charon to bring you to me so that I could shake the hand of the mortal who took down my egomaniacal brother."

"Though we are sorry that you didn't survive the experience," Persephone interjected sympathetically. "What exactly happened up there, anyway?"
"That's what I came to tell you."

Eli took a deep breath and then explained the entire story, from the moment they left Thessaly, to Demeter and Zeus taking their powers and dropping them back at the monastery.

He watched their faces as he told them about Demeter betraying them all; her plans to destroy the Underworld and take Persephone back home for good. Eli could not tell what they were thinking and felt his anxiety worsening with every word he spoke.

Finally, he finished, exhaling a long breath, and waiting for their reactions.

The couple looked at each other once more. This time, Eli realized, they were having an intense and silent conversation, using only their facial expressions to communicate. Persephone gave an exasperated sigh, stepping away from Hades.

"How dare you? That's my mother!"

"Seph, I'm simply saying I believe the boy. What motive would he have to lie?" Hades threw his hands up. "Better yet, what motive does he have to kill himself just so he could come here and lie?"

"Fine, I'll call her here and we can just ask her."

"No!" Eli exclaimed, his teeth chattering. "Please, you have to believe me. They have the weapon, and they could already be on their way any moment, please. I'm not making this up, I swear!"

Eli couldn't help but cry. He felt foolish, but his terror and anguish were too much for him to hold in any longer. Persephone stepped towards him, placing her hand on his shoulder. As soon as Eli felt the warmth, he knew what she was doing. His tears subsided, and he slowed his breathing.

Persephone's deep brown eyes stared into his as if searching for something, widening a moment later as if in realization.

"It can't be." She whispered. "You really are telling the truth."

Eli nodded. Hades wrapped Persephone in a hug as she teared up as well.

"We'll stop this, don't worry." The god stroked her long hair, holding her close to his chest. He looked at Eli. "We need to call the others."

Chapter Twenty-Seven

Eli sat at a long table in Hades' dining room. Hades sat at the head, while Aphrodite, Apollo, and Hermes joined Eli in the middle. Persephone had told Hades she had to go to her room to rest, the weight of her mother's actions heavy on her heart.

"I just can't believe Demeter would do this to us," Aphrodite complained. "What did we ever do to her to deserve it?"

"Well—"

"Oh, shut up, Hades. I know what *you* did." The goddess glared. "But we were her family. But for her to turn on us like this, to have lied right from the start? It's not right."

Hades had spread the news to the remaining gods and invited them to strategize if they were willing to fight. Eli was not very confident about the turnout.

"Where are the others?" Eli asked.

"Well, Dionysus will not be joining us," Hades replied.

"What? Why not?"

"Eli, you must understand," Hermes began.

"Overthrowing Zeus was one thing. Now that Demeter

is working with him as well…"

"It's entirely different." Apollo finished his thought. "Some of us who had chosen a side before are now recalculating our options."

"So, they could side with Demeter." Eli couldn't understand.

Whatever her motivations, the goddess was talking about destroying the entire Underworld. Eli didn't care that her goal was to bring her daughter home. Millions of souls, past and future, would float around in nothingness for eternity, with no way out. It would stop any soul from being able to find peace. How could anyone agree with that?

"They could. In Dionysus's case, though, he became neutral in the fight. To live out the rest of his time, how he sees fit."

"That doesn't help us at all." Eli frowned.

"You said there was a different prophecy than the one we were told?" Aphrodite asked.

"Yes," Eli closed his eyes, "but Zeus only said it once, so I don't fully remember. Most of it was the same, it was only a few lines that were different, about how the truth would tear us apart and that's how Zeus would get the weapon. There was also a line about how we need to find the cracks hidden in the façade or else the Underworld will be destroyed. I'm worried though, that it means we were supposed to see through Demeter's lies before it was too late."

"Interesting." Hades mused.

"We need to go get the rest of the five. I'll bet anything Wyatt memorized the entire thing. Hermes, can you portal me to the monastery?"

Hermes and Hades exchanged a look.

"Eli," Hermes explained slowly, "I can go get them,

but you can't join me. You died. A mortal soul cannot leave the Underworld unless escorted by Hades himself."

"And I," Hades continued, "would not set foot outside of my realm if not for dire circumstances. This is simply a retrieval. Hermes can handle it."

Eli knew that was the risk he was taking when he died, that there was always a chance he wouldn't get back out, but hearing Hermes say it aloud hurt more than he thought it would. He nodded solemnly, hanging his head, and staring at the etchings on the table.

Hermes placed a hand on Eli's shoulder. "I'll be back with them before you know it."

With that, he disappeared.

Just then, a puff of smoke popped into the room, floating towards Hades' head. A Whisper, Eli realized. The wisp circled a few times and then entered the god's ear.

"It's Thanatos, warning us." Hades motioned to the others to follow him. "He has sensed Hephaestus' presence here."

The group followed Hades just outside the front door, stopping at the top of the steps. Eli put his hand up over his brows, peering at a green orb falling from the sky, hurtling towards them.

"Why is he falling so fast?" Aphrodite's voice was concerned. "He can fly. Why isn't he stopping?"

Hephaestus crashed to the ground in front of them, causing an enormous crater in the stone path leading to the castle. The gods rushed forward, while Eli stood frozen.

From where the boy stood, he could see a long gash of blood on Hephaestus' back.

"Brother!" Hades exclaimed, reaching him first.

Hades hoisted the fallen god onto his shoulders, carrying him past Eli and into the foyer. Eli followed them inside and watched Hades set him down on a nearby couch. Hephaestus' face was a sickly gray color, his eyes almost entirely white.

"I didn't know—" Hephaestus coughed up blood as he tried to speak. "I didn't know what she was planning. Please, I'm so sorry."
"Apollo, heal him!"

Apollo rushed forward at Hades' command, placing his hands on his brother's chest.

"This is going to take a few moments. He's not healing as quickly as he should be."

Hephaestus reached out and grabbed his hand.

"I only helped Zeus because I believed the prophecy. I believed the Five would stop him."
"Shh," Apollo reassured him, "It's okay, brother."
"We have little time." Hephaestus choked out the words. "When I came to warn you, they used the knife on me. The blood of the Five. That is the only thing that will stop them. They realized it when Zeus' stab wound did not heal. You must use it on them, or else."

Hephaestus trailed off, falling unconscious as he spoke his last words.

"He's not…" Eli's eyes were wide in shock at the scene.

"Dead? No, just severely injured. The healing is working, it's just very slow going. I can fix him." Apollo kept his hands over Hephaestus. "Hades, take the others and start preparing. Hermes should be back any minute."

Hades rushed Aphrodite and Eli up the stairs, guiding them into a locked room.

"Oh, thank goodness you have weapons." Eli rushed over to a display of swords hanging from the wall.

"Not for you, I'm afraid," Hades smirked, swatting Eli's hand from the blades. "These weapons were used to defeat the Titans. If a dead soul wields them, they could perish. The soul, I mean, not the weapons."

"Then how am I supposed to fight?"

Hades picked up a warrior's helmet from a table nearby, plopping it on Eli's head.

"You're not." He turned the boy towards a mirror, and Eli gasped at the lack of his reflection.

"I'm invisible!"

"And you shall stay that way until we say so, got it?" Aphrodite instructed.

After a moment of silence, she sighed dramatically.

"If you're nodding, we can't see it, Eli."

"Oh, sorry. Yes, I've got it."

"Great," she continued, "and as soon as Liv gets here, I can get my belt back. In the meantime, what have you got for me, Hades?"

The god picked up the sword Eli had been eying.

"This will slice through metal with just a thought. No experience required."

Aphrodite took the hilt with both hands and waved it through the air slowly, getting a feel for the weight.

"Perfect."

Hades smiled at her. He went to one bookshelf and pulled a hardback out. Eli heard a clicking noise and one of the wall panels popped open. From it, Hades pulled out a long metal bident. He held the two-pronged fork fondly, nearly hugging it in his arms. Somehow Eli could feel the energy radiating off of it from where he stood, an ominous and somehow comforting feeling washing over him.

"Can we go now?" Aphrodite rolled her eyes. "It's bad enough that one of us is a murderous traitor. I don't want my last memory of you to be fondling a weapon."

Hades let out a snort. "Hey, at least we're never boring."

Chapter Twenty-Eight

Eli was grateful for his newfound invisibility as he descended the stairs and saw his friends waiting with Hermes. Lucy was more beautiful than he remembered, grumpy face and all. Theo, however, looked downright depressed. His eyes were red as if he had been crying for days. Eli realized then that Theo must have primarily filled his rain cloud, and his heart broke for the boy. Wyatt and Liv were hovering near Apollo, looking concernedly over Hephaestus.

"Well, hello there." Hades greeted them. Aphrodite ran to Liv, pulling her into a tight hug.
"Hades." Lucy acknowledged.

Eli's stomach did a flip at the sound of her voice, and he knew the right thing to do. He sighed and reached for the helmet. Hades reached out a hand to stop him.

"Not until we say so, remember?" Hades muttered through his teeth, providing Eli with a mixed wave of relief and guilt.
"Alright, let's get down to it."

Aphrodite stepped forward and rushed the group through the plan. They would wait for Zeus and Demeter to make their move, steal the knife back, and throw them both into Tartarus.

"How do we get the knife?" Theo asked.
"Unfortunately, we have to play a lot of this by ear. We will figure something out." Aphrodite assured them.

As she walked over to Apollo to check on her brother, Eli finally understood why Hades had given him the helmet.

"I have to steal the knife, don't I?" He whispered.
"You do. And if your friends know, they could give away our position. I sent a Whisper to Hermes, letting him know. He has told your friends that you made it here long enough to warn us, and then took your leave to live out the rest of your afterlife in Elysium."
"And they believed it? I would never leave them like that."
"It is incredible the things mortals will believe, and not believe when they are full of grief." Hades threw a sad smile in Eli's general direction.

The front doors burst open, and the last person Eli needed to see at that moment stepped across the threshold.

"Callie, we don't have time for this." Apollo glared at the woman who had entered.
"Shut it, Apollo. I'm here to help."

■■

Callie walked inside and stood at the center of the foyer. Eli's stomach flipped as he watched the scene unfold, practically in slow motion.

"Hey, isn't that—" Theo jabbed an elbow in Wyatt's side, cutting off his question.

"Yes, Wyatt, Theo." Callie nodded a greeting to them both after seeing the exchange. "It's nice to see you both again. Under worse circumstances, though, I'm afraid."

Liv and Lucy looked at the boys, and then at each other with confused looks on their faces.

"Look, we're a little busy here. Just say what you need to say," Apollo demanded.

"I already did. I'm here to help. I spoke to Clio, and she said this was happening today. So, where do you need me?"

"Anywhere else, preferably."

"Knock it off, Apollo." Aphrodite stepped forward. "Calliope has been my friend longer than she's been your ex. If she wants to help us, then we let her."

Apollo and Callie stared each other down, the tension building between them.

Ex? The word played in Eli's mind, over and over, like a record skipping off the track. Every story he had ever heard of a Greek god finding out someone had been with their lover, ex or not, ran through his head, making him regret ever agreeing to set foot in that bar.

"Calliope." Panic gripped Eli as Wyatt said her name aloud.

Please, Wyatt. Please don't say it.

Eli's prayer was left unanswered.

"Oh, my gods." Wyatt finally put the pieces together. "Waldo made out with a muse?"

The silence that followed was thick and deafening. Eli was sure that if he wasn't already dead, his heart would've stopped.

"I'm sorry. What?" Apollo's voice was low and angry. Eli could tell the god was struggling hard to not look back at where he stood.
"Yeah. Same question." Lucy huffed.
"Look, Lucy, he was really drunk." Theo offered. "And none of the four of you were even together when it happened, for the record."

Hades descended the stairs, Eli quietly in tow.

"We do not have time for this." He commanded. "Calliope, you may stay. We need all the help we can get."

Apollo turned to Hades to object, but one look from the elder god silenced him. He grumbled something angrily under his breath and continued working.

"We have to stop them!" Hephaestus sat up suddenly, coughing and looking around wildly.
"Brother, calm down. You're still healing." Apollo nodded to Wyatt to help restrain the god.
"No, you don't understand. We have to get back to Mount Olympus." Hephaestus broke from and stood tall. "I'm fine enough. We must go. They'll have the weapon completed by now."
Wyatt looked at the god questioningly. "Wasn't the knife supposed to be the weapon?"
"It was only a part of it. Zeus must fasten the knife to a lightning bolt and, once he shoots it into the Underworld, the entire realm will cease to exist. If we stay here, we will cease to exist as well."

"Well, would you look at that?" Hades smirked at Hermes. "Dire circumstances."

Hermes grinned and took a step back, creating a portal in the center of the room. Hades pushed Eli ahead of him through the portal, so as not to draw attention from the others, and everyone else followed. The group arrived on a mound of clouds just outside of the golden gates to Mount Olympus.

Chapter Twenty-Nine

Hades took the lead, Eli staying close to his side at all times. Apollo, Hephaestus, Hermes, and Aphrodite flanked them, while The Five and Callie trailed behind, weapons in hand. Theo carried Eli's old sword, making Eli feel sentimental.

Eli had never realized how hard staying silent was before he could not talk to them. He felt a twinge of nostalgia and thought himself foolish. After all, it had only been a day since they had been in this very spot, huddled up and ready to stop Zeus. But so much had changed in such a short time that it was hard not to feel sentimental.

"Okay, does everyone know their part of the plan?" Hades stopped at the gates and turned to the group before they continued.

"I thought the plan was just barge in, fight, and hopefully win." Theo inquired.

"Good, just making sure we're all on the same page. As soon as anyone sees an opportunity to steal back the weapon, take it."

Liv thrust her hand forward into the center of the group. Eli had to stifle his laughter at the realization of what she was doing.

"What's this?" Hades narrowed his eyes.

Liv looked at Theo and Wyatt. "You guys promised. Well, Eli did, but I'm holding you to it since he's not here."

Wyatt and Theo rolled their eyes, a clear sign of amusement on their faces, and placed their hands on hers.

"Just go with it, it's easier that way," Wyatt instructed everyone else. Once everyone's hands were in the center, Liv grinned.

"All right, 'Go Good Guys!' on three."

■ ■

After making it past the gatekeepers, thanks to Aphrodite and Liv, the group burst through the front doors. Hermes stated to the others that Zeus and Demeter were most likely on the top floor balcony. Since they needed to hoist a lightning bolt at the Underworld, that would be their best vantage point. The group followed him up a winding staircase at the end of the hallway.

As they all reached the top, a hoard of hoplites met them, spears raised in an attack stance. At the front of them stood Ares, sword in hand.

"You're too late, you fools." Ares laughed, haughtily.

Eli wondered if the sneer on his face was a permanent fixture. Perhaps it wasn't a sneer at all, but simply how the god looked. The hall was so quiet that you could hear a pin drop, and the tension was thick in the air as the warring groups assessed each other. Then, finally, a voice broke the silence.

"Who's that guy?"

Wyatt had asked, earning sporadic snorts of laughter from the group of children and gods. Ares turned red in the face and glared at the boy.

"I am Ares. God of—No!" He grunted in frustration. "We just did this two days ago!"
Wyatt wrinkled his nose and made a clicking noise with his tongue. "Are you sure? I think I would remember meeting a God of No We Just Did This Two Days Ago."

"Enough!" Ares raised his sword and gave a signal, prompting the hoplites to rush forward.

Hermes raised his wand, and the hoplites reduced their speed as if they were now trudging through sand. Aphrodite raised her sword and faced Ares head-on.

"Children, take care of the hoplites." She instructed the remaining Five. "Brothers, I'll need your help here."

Apollo raised his bow as well, signaling to Hades.

"Go, Hades! We'll take care of these half-wits."

Hades ducked and dodged through the sounds of weapons clashing against one another. Eli followed his path exactly and ran to catch up with him once he was through.

"I can't see you and you can't speak," Hades whispered. "So, I'm saying this on a wing and a prayer that you're with me. Stay silent, and act only on my signal."

Eli reached his hand out and touched the god's arm in assurance. Hades gave a small nod, and they continued.

Hades led them into an enormous ballroom, with columns lining the walls, and a set of glass doors leading out onto a balcony. Through the glass door, they could see Zeus and Demeter standing out on the oversized deck. Hades flung the doors open, just as Zeus finished fastening the knife to the bolt.

"Zeus!" Hades' voice was loud and commanding, echoing throughout the skies.

Demeter and Zeus looked up at him, smug smiles on their faces. Zeus raised his hand, aiming the bolt at the ground.

"Ah, big brother. Just in time to watch the show." Zeus sneered. "I have to admit, I would've preferred you had a front-row seat from your home, but this will work just as well."

"Zeus, Demeter, please. You don't have to do this."

"Oh, shut up Hades." Demeter scowled. "Of course, we have to do this. It's not a moral dilemma. You stole my daughter from me. If this is the only way to get her back, and for you to be punished, then so be it."

"I didn't steal her," Hades countered. "Persephone and I love each other. She chose to stay with me."

"Enough of this nonsense," Zeus interrupted, to no avail.

"Then where is she now? Certainly not standing by your side." Demeter continued. "If she wasn't a prisoner, why could she not be here to tell me that herself?"

"You should be lucky she's not here. You would both already be dead."

It surprised Eli to hear the amusement and pride in Hades' voice, considering it was such a threatening statement.

"How dare you? She's my daughter, and you've been keeping her a hostage."

"You know that's not how it works, sister. She consumed the seeds in the Underworld. She can only leave it when the land allows her to, not me. If it were up to me, she would come and go as she pleases. I swear on my life Demeter, I would give her the world if I could."

"And that is why the Underworld will no longer be an issue." Demeter grinned wickedly. "Cut out the middleman, right?"

"Demeter, please, why not stop this now?" Hades took a step closer. "We can figure this out together."

"Enough of this foolishness." Zeus interrupted, scowling at Hades.

The god gave a wave of his hand and Hades cried out, stumbling backwards. Blood began dripping off of his jacket. He clutched his chest and opened his shirt revealing several stab wounds.

During the interaction, Eli had been quietly inching his way towards the lightning bolt. He now stood directly behind Zeus, waiting impatiently for Hades' signal. He glanced up to see the rest of the group had also arrived, bruised, and bloodied, all watching the scene from the doorway. Zeus realized as well, and he slammed the doors shut with a wave of his arm. Both Apollo and Hermes yanked at the door handle, but it refused to budge.

"Brother, please–" Hades pleaded.

"No! I said enough!"

The clouds began to darken, several bolts of lightning flickering and lighting up the skies.

"You always came out on top." Zeus shouted over a cacophony of thunder. "You were the key to defeating our father. You found true love. I sent you to the Underworld, and you made it a home for lost souls everywhere. Even after all the false tales I planted to our followers, painting you as the Devil, you were still everyone's favorite. And now?"

Zeus lifted the weapon once more, aiming it back at the ground and laughing menacingly.

"Now, you will be nothing."

"Go, now!" Hades cried out.

Eli leapt from behind Zeus, knocking the weapon out of his hands.

"What the—" Zeus turned and swatted at the air, trying to find the invisible force that had attacked him.

As the boy leaned down to retrieve the weapon, Zeus made contact, punching so hard that the helmet flew off of Eli's head, and he was completely visible again.

"You insolent swine!" Zeus roared.

The god leaned down to grab the bolt, swiping it out from under Eli and lifting his arm. In the blink of an eye, the bolt was gone, hurtling itself downwards towards the Underworld.

"No!" Eli cried out and did the only thing he could think of to do. He jumped.

As he fell, he used every bit of strength he had to contort his body into a nosedive position. Pinning his arms to his sides, he sped up neck and neck with the deadly weapon. He stretched his arm as far as it would go, crying out as he finally grabbed the projectile.

The bolt burned in his hand, searing at his skin so badly that he nearly dropped it, but Eli gritted his teeth and held on tightly, tucking it into his arms so that he was falling under it. He squeezed his eyes shut and waited for the impact, hoping that since he was already dead, he wouldn't die again.

After a few moments passed, Eli started to feel strange. There was no longer any wind whipping past him, he felt still, light somehow. He opened one eye slowly, peering around himself. Both eyelids flew open when he realized he was no longer falling at all.

He was flying.

Eli laughed, still clutching the burning bolt tightly, and urged himself to float higher, whizzing through the air and back onto the balcony. He landed strongly with both feet on the ground.

"Hey! Douchebag!" He called to Zeus. "You dropped your lightening."
"Eli?" Demeter's jaw dropped. "How?"

Zeus outstretched his arms upwards furiously. As he let out a scream, a strand of lightning from the clouds entered the god's arm and shot outwards towards the boy. Eli dodged to the right, and the bolt struck Hades right in the chest, causing him to fall forward on the ground, unmoving.

Eli could hear the cries from their cohorts still in the ballroom, his heart pounding. Eli gripped the lightning bolt tighter, embracing the pain he held in his palm. He turned to Zeus, his eyes narrowed and darkened.

With a cry filled with pain, rage, and frustration, Eli raised the bolt and heaved it at the god. As the lightning made an impact, Zeus' eyes went wide with shock. The bolt stuck into the god's chest, and blood dripped from the corners of his mouth. Zeus fell forward, cracking the ground beneath him with a loud thud.

"You killed him." Demeter gasped. "That's impossible."

The doors to the ballroom flew open, everyone rushing out to Hades' side. Eli pried his eyes away from Zeus' corpse and looked at his friends, swallowing hard at their expressions. Theo and Liv held looks of awe. Wyatt simply nodded to Eli before focusing his attention on Hades.

Lucy, however, was intense. Her eyes narrowed in anger. She looked away from Eli, focusing instead on Hades as well, and Eli felt a pain deep in his chest. He knew she would be furious with him, but at that moment, he also knew he had hurt her. A feeling he had never wanted to make her feel.

Apollo flipped Hades over and placed his hands on his chest. Aphrodite turned and buried her head in Hermes' shoulder, sobbing when Hades did not wake.

"Please, tell me he's breathing," Demeter whispered to Apollo.

"Demeter." Hermes' voice was gravelly and cold. "You need to leave. Now."

Demeter opened her mouth as if to argue, but snapped it shut just as quickly. She gave a small nod and fled from the balcony.

As Eli watched Hades, a warm feeling spread through him, like rays of sunshine filling his insides.

Eli went to Hades and knelt involuntarily. He was not acting with thought but was being driven by the warm feeling in his gut. He placed his hands on top of Apollo's and thought of the caterpillars.

He had squeezed his eyes so tightly in focus that he didn't understand why he heard a collective gasp around him, but he did not open them to look around. He, instead, concentrated on satiating the growing urge inside of him. An urge that simply told him he had to help.

"I don't understand." Hermes' voice whispered.
"How is he doing that?" Aphrodite joined in.

Eli felt a sense of calm washing over him and finally let go, opening his eyes and seeing Hades staring back at him. Eli stood and looked up at the shocked faces surrounding him.

"What?" He asked them. The collective continued to gape.
Finally, Theo stammered out the words. "Bro, you're glowing."

Eli looked down at his hands and, sure enough, they were emitting a glowing, golden aura. He sucked in a breath, his head filling with questions, but only one came out.

"Why?"
"You saved us all." Hades rose to his feet. "Just

holding that lightning bolt should have killed you. You have proven yourself to the heavens, and now you are one of us."

Chapter Thirty

Every so often, we find ourselves thinking we're at the right place at the right time. For the first time in his life, Elias Riley could agree with the notion. With his new power, he was immortal. He had saved the world and the Underworld, but something still didn't feel right. He did not do it alone, and that fact was weighing on his mind.

After they had defeated Zeus, Hermes used a portal to take Lucy back to the hospital she had left Damien in. According to Hermes, it was a touching reunion. Once Damien had completely healed, they took him back home to Nevada.

Lucy and Hermes returned to Hades' home with a large box addressed to Liv. There were several holes in the sides and the box sported a giant red bow. Liv opened it to find the dodo bird they had left on the island. Shrieking with glee, she immediately went to work finding food and blankets for it.

"Can it survive in the Underworld?" Wyatt had asked Hermes.

"I mean, it's already extinct, right?" Hermes had

shrugged back at him.

"Please don't let her feed it here," Hades interjected. "I already take care of Cerberus; I don't need another pet."

Without Zeus to protect him, the remaining gods seized Ares. Instead of a cell in Tartarus, however, Apollo decided Sisyphus deserved a break, and he put Ares in charge of rolling the boulder up the hill instead.

The group had all returned to Hades' castle in the Underworld. Dionysus, Athena, Artemis, and Poseidon even joined them as well. They sat in the dining room and celebrated, the Five recounting the tales of their journey to the gods.

Eli couldn't help but notice how well Lucy and Callie were getting along and was slightly confused. He leaned over to nudge Liv.

"What's the deal there?"

"Oh, that." Liv laughed as she realized what Eli was asking. "So, during our part of the battle, there was only one hoplite left, and Callie and Lucy both went for it at the same time. The hoplite ducked out of the way, so they both just started fighting each other. I guess it was a bonding experience for them though because they've been thick as thieves ever since they stopped. Callie's awesome, by the way. Great find."

Eli chuckled at Liv's explanation and glanced back at Lucy, completely floored by how constantly she still surprised him.

Apollo listened in awe as Wyatt told everyone about the anthropophage attack. Aphrodite laughed along with Liv as she told the story of how she essentially stole a boat for them. And Hermes couldn't contain himself after Lucy reminisced about punting Chicken Eli off the boat while battling the sirens.

"Yo, dudes," Poseidon laughed loudly. "You gotta tell the one again about the chicken riding the Pegasus, man."

Eli excused himself as the table erupted in laughter, smiling as well so that no one thought he was leaving in anger at the god's comment. He still had not spoken to his friends, to Lucy. Even though he was now indestructible, he felt as if he was having trouble breathing.

He stepped outside the front door, taking in a deep breath, and overlooking the city. He kept waiting to feel differently, now that he was a god, but he still felt exactly the same. The only difference he had noted so far was the intense guilt he felt over taking a life, no matter how evil that life had been.

The cosmos circled above his head, and the entire experience felt surreal. As if it was happening to someone else. He wanted to kick himself. This was everything he had ever wanted, and now that he had it, it felt wrong somehow.

"Elias?"

The voice startled Eli, and he reflexively reached for his sword. Looking in the distance, he saw Demeter walking up the pathway and kept his hand on the hilt.

"You shouldn't be here."
"I just need a moment. Please."

Against his better judgment, Eli nodded at the goddess to continue.

"I just wanted to say," she began, unsurely, "I am deeply apologetic for my behavior towards you. Towards all of you. I do not expect your forgiveness, but I hope you can someday understand my motives."

"I do understand." Eli replied, thinking carefully before continuing, "And, I appreciate your apology, but I can't accept it, and I hope you can accept that."

"Eli…"

"With all due respect, you're only trying to make amends now because Zeus is dead, and you're scared." His voice grew angrier with every word. "You were still willing to destroy everything. Millions of lives. I looked at you like family. You were my mentor. Regardless of your motives, I can never trust you again."

"I did what I did out of love for my daughter." Demeter's voice was sad and defeated, but Eli could not allow himself to feel compassion for her.

"Then I truly hope I never love someone that much," Eli replied coldly, and he turned his back on her as she had done to him.

He went back inside, leaning against the door after it had closed.

"Why so glum, chum?" Hades joined Eli in the foyer. "Just letting something go."

Eli shook off the subject, not wanting to get into the details of his conversation with Demeter. He knew he had spoken out of anger, but that was all he felt towards her. Maybe one day, he would see it from her point of view. For now, he just wanted to avoid thinking about it.

"You know, it's really not fair." Eli mused to Hades. "I didn't do any of this alone. Why did my friends not get their powers back too?"

"I do not pretend to understand how the heavens work," Hades replied. "Perhaps it was because you were the one who delivered the final blow to Zeus. No one has ever killed a god before, so this is uncharted territory for all of us. It could very well be that they simply wanted a replacement as King of the Gods."

"I don't want to be a King," Eli said slowly.

After all of his insecurities and anxieties about being special, a chosen one, it was only then that he realized that was never what he truly wanted.

Hades gave him a reassuring smile. "I know. And you don't have to be. The one thing I do know about the universe is that it does not take away what it has given. You can do as you choose with your newfound powers. I would strongly advise, though, that you do not return to your previous life. While you can hide your aura, it is dangerous to pretend you are the same as you once were."

"I wouldn't want to go home, either. But I don't know where I would go."

Eli looked up and saw Lucy appear in the doorway. Hades patted the boy on the shoulder.

"I'll give you two a moment. Maybe she can help with that."

Lucy's face had softened since Eli had seen her on the balcony. It no longer seemed like she wanted to punch him in the face, and while Eli felt relief, he kept his guard up, just in case.

"Hello, your excellency," Lucy bowed sarcastically and smirked as she rose.

Eli shook his head. "I prefer Waldo, honestly."

"Waldo it is, then."

The pair stood in silence for a moment, awkwardly. Finally, Eli took a deep breath and found the courage to speak.

"I'm sorry."

"I know." Lucy nodded. "I'm still pissed off if I'm being honest. But you forgave me for helping Zeus. I suppose I can forgive you for kissing another girl, literally killing yourself, leaving us all behind, making Theo cry for a whole day, hiding when—"

"Alright, alright, I get it," Eli chuckled, cutting her off. "I said I was sorry."

"Apology accepted." She grinned, shoving him lightly. "Don't do it again, jackass."

Eli closed the distance between them, pulling her into a tight hug.

He buried his head in her hair and mumbled, "I missed you."

As he let go, Lucy's hand found its way to the nape of his neck, pulling his head downwards towards hers. As their lips touched, Eli felt the same energy that he had felt the first time they met, when Lucy had woken him up. It was like pin pricks and tingles throughout his body. Eli wrapped his arms around her, clinging to her tightly.

"Again, gross," Eli broke away, laughing at Liv's quip.

He turned to see Theo, Wyatt, and Liv coming towards them, all giggling. As they reached the pair, Lucy took a step away from Eli, throwing him a wink.

"So, we're gonna go to Denny's for a 'Congrats on Saving the Universe' party. Dionysus is renting out the whole place for us. You guys down?" Wyatt asked them.

"Ooh, can Callie come, too?" Lucy asked.

"Seriously?"

"Well, if Eli got to kiss her, I should get a chance to kiss her too. That's the backbone of any healthy relationship, Wyatt."

"Alright, Alright," Wyatt shrugged off Lucy's sarcasm.

"On that note," Eli cleared his throat. "I'm glad you're all here. I just wanted to say—"

"We already know you're sorry, Waldo," Theo assured him. "But you saved the world, so we forgive you."

"Thanks." Eli smiled.

"Had you failed," Liv interjected, "we would have never spoken to you again."

"Because we would all be dead, of course." Wyatt clarified.

Eli laughed and nodded, grateful that out of everyone, the universe decided these were the friends he should get to have.

"Alright, let's get going," Wyatt said. "I'm ready to see Lucy's face when they're out of waffles again."

Lucy laughed and gave Wyatt a playful shove. Her eyes went wide, and she slapped a hand over her mouth as the boy flew across the room, landing in a potted plant.

"Did I—" she looked questioningly at Eli.

"You did." Eli narrowed his eyes in confusion, trying not to laugh at how Wyatt had flailed.

"But how?"

"Maybe it's because Eli kissed you?" Liv wondered.

"If that's the case, can he kiss me, too?" Wyatt called from the ground.

Eli walked over to help him up.

"I do wonder." Eli began as the boys returned to the group, deciding to try something.

He held out his hand and nodded to the others to place their hands on his. As if an electric current was racing through his veins, Eli shivered. He could tell the others were re-awakening by the looks on their faces.

Not only that, but Eli's aura spread to their arms, creating a bright glow of their own.

"Holy shit." Theo gawked. "We've got our powers back!"
"And we have auras now. Does that mean—?" Liv trailed off, looking at Wyatt.
"We're all gods now," Wyatt answered, looking down at his glowing fingers.

The elder gods rushed out into the foyer upon hearing the commotion. Each ancestor hugged their descendant in congratulations while Hades and Persephone stood near Eli, looking proudly at him. He had always thought that all he needed was to be special, a hero. But looking around at everyone in the room, thinking back over the past few days, Eli finally understood what he had truly been searching for. At that moment, he knew that this was all he needed and all he would ever need.

A found, somewhat broken, yet wholly unconditional love that could only come from a genuine family.

Epilogue

Demeter strolled through her garden, admiring the sunrise over the hills that surrounded her home. She took a deep breath, inhaling the scent of the lilies from the nearby bushes.

As soon as she had fled from speaking with Eli, she returned to her home, fully aware that her time here was coming to an end.

"Mother."

As if on cue, she heard the voice from behind her. Tears welled up in Demeter's eyes, her body frozen in place, unable to face her daughter.

"Mother," Persephone said again. "I just want to speak with you."

"I'm no fool, Persephone." Demeter finally forced herself to turn, looking straight into the young goddesses' eyes. "You're not here to speak, they've sent you to arrest me."

"Please," Persephone frowned. "It doesn't have to be this way. It's not too late, you can say you're sorry—"

"Sorry?" Demeter let out a harsh laugh. "But I'm not. I did what I needed to do, to save you, to bring you home. I will not apologize for that."

Persephone's eyes widened. She took a small step backward, a look of shock on her face.

"You would've destroyed an entire realm. Countless souls, past present, and future. Can't you see how insane that is?"

"I did it for you!" Demeter cried, incredulously. "To bring you back to me, so we could be a family again!"

With a sharp exhale, Persephone's brows narrowed.

"I was in the Underworld when he was planning on destroying it. It's odd to me that you never factored that into your grand scheme."

"Zeus told me he was sending Ares to retrieve you. He's your father, and he wanted to do right by you."

"He's never done right by any woman in his life, why on earth did you believe he would start with us?" Persephone exclaimed, throwing her hands in the air. "No one was coming for me. Ares wasn't sent on a rescue mission; he was sent into battle."

Demeter shook her head, unwilling to fall prey to her daughter's delusions. A burning sensation in her gut rose up creating bile in her throat.

"Hades has influenced you beyond my reach, it seems." She sneered. "I will not apologize."

"Then I have no choice," Persephone lifted her hand.

"Fine, daughter, have it your way." Demeter stepped away. "You want to call me a villain, so be it."

With one last maniacal laugh, Demeter waved her hands and vanished, leaving Persephone alone in the garden.

THE END

Made in United States
North Haven, CT
04 August 2022

22273521R00134